Fvp

Maigret and the Madwoman

Georges Simenon

Maigret and the Madwoman

Translated from the French by Eileen Ellenbogen

A Harvest Book • Harcourt, Inc.

A Helen and Kurt Wolff Book

Orlando Austin New York San Diego Toronto London

Library of Congress Cataloguing-in-Publication Data
Simenon, Georges, 1903–1989.
Maigret and the Madwoman
(A Harvest book)
"A Helen and Kurt Wolff book."
Translation of La folle de Maigret.
I. Title.
PZ3.S5892Maegqn 1979   [PQ2637.I53]
843'.9'12   79-10401
ISBN 0-15-602850-6

Printed in the United States of America
First Harvest edition 1979

A C E G I J H F D B

Maigret and the Madwoman

Chapter 1

Flanking the main gate of Police Headquarters, Officer Picot stood guard on the left, and his old friend Latuile on the right. It was about ten o'clock on a fine morning in May. The sunlight was dazzling, and Paris was aglow with color, like a pastel drawing.

Picot could not have said exactly when he first noticed her. It did not seem important at the time. She was a tiny old woman, in a white hat, white cotton gloves, and a dress of gun-metal gray. Her legs were very thin and slightly bowed with age.

Had she been carrying a shopping basket or a handbag? He could not remember. He had not been aware of her approach. She was only a few feet away from him, standing on the sidewalk, peering at the rows of little cars parked in the forecourt of Police Headquarters.

Not that sightseers were uncommon at the Quai des Orfèvres, but mostly they were tourists. She drew nearer, went right up to the gate, inspected one of the policemen

3

from top to toe, then turned and made off in the direction of the Pont-Neuf.

Picot was on duty again the following morning, and at about the same time as on the previous day he saw her once more. This time, after some considerable hesitation, she came up and spoke to him.

"This is the place where Chief Superintendent Maigret has his office, isn't it?"

"Yes, madame. On the second floor."

She raised her head and gazed up at the windows. She had very delicate, finely modeled features, and her clear gray eyes had a look of permanent puzzlement.

"Thank you, Officer."

She went on her way with little mincing steps. This time he noticed that she was carrying a string shopping bag, which would seem to indicate that she lived somewhere nearby.

On the third day Picot was off duty. His replacement paid no attention to the little old woman, who sidled through into the forecourt. She wandered around for a minute or two and then went in through the door on the left and began climbing the stairs. On the second floor she stopped and peered down the long corridor, apparently feeling a little lost.

Old Joseph, the messenger, went up to her and asked, in his friendly way, if he could be of any assistance.

"I'm looking for Chief Superintendent Maigret's office."

"Do you wish to see the Chief Superintendent?"

"Yes. That's what I'm here for."

"Do you have an appointment?"

Looking very downcast, she shook her head.

"Can't I see him without an appointment?"

"Would you care to leave a message?"

"I must speak to him personally. It's terribly important."

"If you'll fill in one of these forms, I'll see if the Chief Superintendent can see you."

She sat down at a table covered with a green baize cloth. They had just had the decorators in, and the whole building smelled strongly of paint. Unaware of this, she was struck by the cheerful look of things: not at all what one would have expected of a Government Department.

Having filled in one form, she then proceeded to tear it up. She wrote slowly, composing her sentences with great care and underlining a word here and there. A second form followed the first into the wastepaper basket, and then a third. It was not until after her fourth attempt that she appeared satisfied. She went over to Joseph with the form.

"You'll see that it's handed to him personally, won't you?"

"Yes, madame."

"He's probably very busy."

"Very."

"Do you think he'll see me?"

"I couldn't say, madame."

She was at least eighty-five, eighty-six or seven perhaps, and as light and slender as a girl. Age had fined her down, and her delicate skin was translucent. She looked up at Joseph, goodhearted fellow that he was, and gave him a shy smile, anxious to win him over.

"You will do your best, won't you? It's so terribly important to me!"

"Take a seat, madame."

He went up to one of the doors and knocked. Maigret

was in conference with Janvier and Lapointe, who were both standing by the window, which was wide open, letting in all the hubbub of the street outside.

Maigret took the form from Joseph, glanced at it, and frowned.

"What's she like?"

"A very respectable old lady. A little shy. She was most insistent that she see you."

On the dotted line at the top of the form she had written her name in a surprisingly firm, neat hand:

Madame Antoine de Caramé

And below, the address:

8B Quai de la Mégisserie

She stated as the object of her visit:

The caller has something of the utmost importance to communicate to Chief Superintendent Maigret. It is a matter of life and death.

Here the handwriting was more shaky and the words irregularly spaced. "Chief Superintendent" and "utmost importance" were underlined. "A matter of life and death" was underscored twice.

"Is she mad?" muttered Maigret, sucking at his pipe.

"That isn't how she strikes me. She seems very quiet and composed."

Everyone at the Quai des Orfèvres had at some time or other had to deal with letters from lunatics or cranks, and the underlining of words was a characteristic of most of them.

"You'd better see her, Lapointe. Unless someone does, we'll have her calling here every day."

A few minutes later the old woman was ushered into the little office at the back. Lapointe was waiting there alone, standing near the window.

"Please come in, madame. Take a seat."

She looked him up and down in some bewilderment. "Are you his son?"

"Whose son?"

"The Chief Superintendent's."

"No, madame. My name is Inspector Lapointe."

"But you're only a boy!"

"I'm twenty-seven."

And so he was. Nevertheless, he didn't look a day over twenty-two and was more like most people's idea of a student than a police officer.

"It was Chief Superintendent Maigret I asked to see."

"Unfortunately he can't spare the time at the moment."

She hesitated, standing in the doorway, fidgeting with her white handbag, uncertain whether to stay or go.

"What if I were to come back tomorrow?"

"He still couldn't see you."

"Doesn't Chief Superintendent Maigret ever grant interviews?"

"Only in very special cases."

"Mine is a very special case. Just that. It's a matter of life and death."

"So you said on the form."

"Well, then?"

"If you will tell me what it's all about, I'll report to the Chief and let him be the judge."

"Do you think he might agree to see me?"

"I can't promise, but he very well might."

She remained standing for quite some time, pondering the pros and cons, and then, apparently having made up her mind, sat down on the edge of a chair facing Lapointe, who was now seated at the desk.

"What's the trouble?"

"I should explain, first of all, that I've lived in the same apartment on the Quai de la Mégisserie for the past forty-two years. On the ground floor there's a man who sells birds. In the summer, when he puts all the cages out on the sidewalk, I can hear them all day long. It's company for me."

"You said you were in some sort of danger, I think."

"I'm in danger all right, but I suppose you think I'm driveling. The young always seem to imagine that old people aren't quite right in the head."

"No such thought ever occurred to me."

"I don't quite know how to put this. My second husband died twelve years ago, and since then I've been by myself in the apartment, and no one but me ever has a reason to go into it. It's too big for me now, really, but I've set my heart on living my time out there. I'm eighty-six, and I can still manage the cooking and housework without any help."

"Do you keep a pet? A dog or a cat?"

"No. As I said, I can always hear the birds singing. My apartment is on the second floor, just above the shop."

"What is it that's worrying you?"

"It's hard to say. At least four times in the past two weeks, I've noticed that my things have been moved."

"What do you mean? Are you saying that after you've

8

been out, you've come back to find your things disturbed?"

"That's right. A frame hanging slightly crooked or a vase turned around. That sort of thing."

"Are you quite sure?"

"There you are, you see! Because I'm an old woman, you think I'm wandering in my wits. I did tell you, don't forget, that I've lived forty-two years in that same apartment. Naturally, if anything is out of place, I spot it at once."

"Has anything been stolen? Have you missed anything?"

"No, Inspector."

"Do you keep money in the apartment?"

"Very little. Just enough to meet my monthly expenses. My first husband was in local government. I still draw a pension from City Hall. Besides that I have a Post Office Savings Account."

"Do you have valuables, jewelry, art objects, anything of that sort?"

"I have things that are of value to me, but I doubt if they're worth much in terms of cash."

"Were there any other signs of an intruder, such as a damp footprint, for instance?"

"There hasn't been a drop of rain for the past ten days."

"Cigarette ashes?"

"No."

"Have you ever given anyone a key to your apartment?"

"No. I have the only key, and I always keep it in my bag."

It was difficult for him to conceal his embarrassment.

"In other words, all it amounts to is that, from time to time, you find some of your things not precisely as you left them?"

"That's right."

"You've never caught any unauthorized person in the apartment?"

"Never."

"And you don't have any idea who the intruder might be?"

"None."

"Do you have any children?"

"Much to my sorrow, I never had a child."

"Any other relations?"

"One niece. She's a masseuse. I don't see her very often, though she doesn't live far from me, just across the river."

"What about friends? Men friends, women friends?"

"Most of the people I used to know are dead. And there's something else, too."

She said it quite casually. There was no underlying note of hysteria, and her bright glance never wavered.

"I'm being followed."

"In the street, you mean?"

"Yes."

"Have you actually seen the person who's following you?"

"Whenever I stop suddenly and look back there's someone there, but not always the same person. I don't know who it can be."

"Do you go out much?"

"Every morning. I go out at about eight to do my shopping. I miss Les Halles very much, now that they've been moved. It was so convenient, just around the corner, and old habits die hard. Since then I've shopped around a bit locally, but it will never be the same."

"Is it a man who's following you?"

"I don't know."

"I presume you get back at about ten?"

"Thereabouts. And then I sit by the window and shell peas, or whatever."

"Do you stay in, in the afternoon?"

"Only when the weather's bad. I like to get a bit of fresh air whenever I can. Usually I sit on a park bench, preferably in the Tuileries Gardens. I have my own favorite bench. I'm not the only one. People of my age are like that, you know. I see the same old faces there, year in, year out."

"Are you followed as far as the Tuileries?"

"Only part of the way, so he can make sure I won't be coming back right away, I think."

"Have you ever done that?"

"Three times. I pretended I'd forgotten something and turned back."

"And, needless to say, you found no one there?"

"That doesn't alter the fact that on other occasions my things have been moved. Someone has it in for me, though I can't think why. I've never done any harm to anyone. There may be more than one person involved."

"You said your husband was in local government. What did he do?"

"He was the Council Clerk. He had very heavy responsibilities. Unfortunately, he died young, of a heart attack. He was just forty-five."

"And you married again?"

"Not till almost ten years later. My second husband was chief buyer at the Hôtel de Ville department store. He was in charge of agricultural implements and tools in general."

"Is he dead, too?"

"He'd been retired for some years when he died. If he'd lived, he'd have been ninety-two."

"When did he die?"

"I thought I told you. Twelve years ago."

"Did he have any family? Was he a widower when you married him?"

"He had only one son. He lives in Venezuela."

"I'll tell you what, madame. I'd better go and report all you've just told me to the Chief Superintendent."

"Do you think he'll agree to see me?"

"If he does, he'll get in touch with you."

"Do you have my address?"

"It's on the form you filled in, isn't it?"

"That's true, I'd forgotten. The thing is, you see, I think the world of him. It seems to me he's the only one who could possibly understand. I don't mean any disrespect to you, but you do seem a bit on the young side to me."

He accompanied her to the door and down the long corridor to the top of the main staircase.

When he got back to Maigret's office, Janvier was no longer there.

"Well?"

"I think you're right, Chief. She must be a bit cracked. All the same, you wouldn't think so. She's very soft-spoken, very cool and self-possessed. She's eighty-six, and all I can say is, I hope I'll be as alert as she is when I get to be her age."

"What about this threat or whatever it is that's hanging over her head?"

"She's lived in the same apartment on the Quai de la Mégisserie for more than forty years. She's been married twice. She claims that, while she's out, some of her things get moved."

Maigret relit his pipe.

"What sorts of things?"

"Picture frames hanging crooked, vases turned back to front..."

"Does she have a dog or a cat?"

"No. She makes do with birdsong. Apparently there's a man who sells birds on the ground floor."

"Anything else?"

"Yes. She was convinced that she's being followed."

"Has she actually seen anyone following her?"

"No, that's just it. But she seems to have an obsession about it."

"Will she be coming back?"

"She's set her heart on seeing you personally. She talks about you as if you were the Good Lord Himself. You're the only one, it seems, who could possibly understand. What should I do?"

"Nothing."

"She's sure to be back."

"We'll cross that bridge when we come to it. Meanwhile, you might go to have a word with the concierge."

Maigret turned his attention once more to the file that he had been reading, and young Lapointe went back to the inspectors' duty room.

"Was she a nut case?" Janvier asked.

"Probably, but a very unusual one."

"Do you know many nut cases?"

"One of my aunts is a patient in a mental hospital."

"The old girl seems to have made quite an impression on you."

"She did, in a way. To her I'm just a kid, who couldn't possibly understand her problem. She's pinned all her hopes on Maigret."

That same afternoon Lapointe strolled along the Quai de la Mégisserie, where almost every shopwindow was filled with birds and other small pets. Because of the glorious weather, there were tables and chairs on the sidewalk outside every café. When he got to number 8B, Lapointe looked up at the second-floor windows and saw that they were wide open. He had some difficulty in finding the lodge, which was across a courtyard at the back of the building. The concierge was sitting in a patch of sunlight darning a pair of men's socks.

"Looking for anyone in particular?"

He showed her his official card.

"I'd be grateful for anything you could tell me about Madame Antoine de Caramé. That is her name, isn't it, the old lady who lives on the second floor?"

"I know, I know. Actually, Antoine was her second husband's surname, so legally her name is Madame Antoine. But she's very proud of her first husband, who was something quite high up in city government, so she likes to be known as Madame Antoine de Caramé."

"What do you make of her?"

"What do you mean?"

"Is she at all peculiar?"

"What I want to know is why the police are taking such an interest in her all of a sudden."

"She came asking for our help."

"What seems to be the trouble?"

"Apparently things get moved around in her apartment while she's out. Hasn't she said anything to you?"

"She just asked me if I'd seen any strangers going up there. I said I hadn't. I wouldn't anyway, not from here. I can't see the front entrance or the staircase."

"Does she have many visitors?"

"Only her niece, who comes once or twice a month. And even she sometimes doesn't show up for three months at a stretch."

"Have you ever noticed anything odd about her behavior?"

"She's very much like any other old woman living by herself. She's a real lady, you can see that, and she's always very polite to everyone."

"Is she at home now?"

"No. She never misses a chance of sunning herself on her favorite bench in the Tuileries."

"Does she talk to you at all?"

"Just a few words when we happen to meet. Most of the time she inquires about my husband, who's in the hospital."

"I'm much obliged to you."

"I take it you'd rather I didn't mention your visit?"

"It doesn't matter one way or the other."

"At any rate, I don't think she's mad, if that's what you're getting at. She has her quirks—all old people do—but no more than anyone else."

"You may be seeing me again."

Maigret was in high spirits. For ten days there hadn't been a drop of rain, the pale blue sky was cloudless, and a gentle breeze was blowing. In this perfect spring weather, Paris was as gay and colorful as a backdrop in an operetta.

He stayed rather late in his office to check through a report, which he had been working on for some time and was anxious to get rid of. He could hear the passing traffic, cars and buses, and occasionally a tug on the river sounding its horn.

It was nearly seven when he opened the door to the inspectors' room to tell Lucas and the two or three other inspectors on night duty that he was leaving.

He went downstairs, toying with the idea of dropping in at the Brasserie Dauphine for an apéritif. As he went out through the main gate, he exchanged greetings with the two officers on guard.

After a moment or two of hesitation, he decided that he would rather go straight home. He had gone a few yards in the direction of the Boulevard du Palais when the tiny figure of a woman stepped into his path. He had no difficulty in recognizing her from Lapointe's description.

"It really is you, isn't it?" she said with great fervor.

She saw no need to address him by name. Whom could she mean but the great, the famous Chief Superintendent, every detail of whose cases she had read avidly in the newspapers? She even went so far as to paste into scrapbooks every word that was written about him.

"Please forgive me for stopping you in the street like this, but in there they wouldn't let me near you."

Maigret felt a little foolish. He could just imagine the two policemen exchanging amused glances behind his back.

"Mind you, I can see their point. I don't hold it against them. After all, it's their job to see that you're not disturbed when you're busy, isn't it?"

It was her eyes that made the deepest impression on the Chief Superintendent: clear, light-gray eyes, very gentle and yet full of sparkle. She smiled at him. Clearly, she was in seventh heaven. But there was something else about her, an intense vitality, quite extraordinary in such a tiny woman.

"Which way are you going?"

He pointed toward the Pont Saint-Michel.

"Would you mind very much if I walked with you?"

Trotting along at his side, she seemed even tinier.

"The main thing is, do you see, that you should realize I'm not mad. I know how we old people look to the young, and I am a very old woman indeed."

"You're eighty-six, aren't you?"

"I see that the young man I spoke to has told you all about me. He seems very young for the job, but you can see he's been well brought up. He has beautiful manners."

"Have you been waiting here long?"

"Since five or six. I thought you left your office at six. I saw a great many gentlemen come out, but you weren't among them."

So she had stood there waiting a whole hour, ignored by the two indifferent policemen on guard duty.

"I have this feeling that I'm in danger. Someone is sneaking into my apartment and rummaging through my things. There must be some reason for it."

"You say someone has been searching your apartment. How do you know?"

"Because I find things not quite as I left them. I'm extremely tidy. It's almost an obsession. In my apartment, there's a place for everything, and for more than forty years everything has been in its place."

"And this has happened more than once?"

"At least four times."

"Do you have anything valuable?"

"No, Chief Superintendent. Nothing but the sorts of odds

and ends that one accumulates over the years and keeps for reasons of sentiment."

She stopped suddenly and looked back over her shoulder.

"Is anyone following you now?" he asked.

"Not at this moment, no. I beg you to come and see me. You'll understand it all much better when I've shown you the place."

"I'll do my best to try to fit it in."

"For an old woman like me, can't you do better than that? The Quai de la Mégisserie is just around the corner from here. Drop in to see me sometime in the next day or so. I promise I won't keep you. And I promise I won't bother you at your office again."

She was nothing if not artful.

"I'll come as soon as I can."

"This week?"

"This week, if possible. Otherwise, early next week."

They had arrived at his bus stop.

"Please forgive me. I must be on my way home now."

"I'm relying on you. I trust you."

At that moment, he would have found it hard to say what he really felt about her. There was no denying that she might have made the whole thing up. That, at any rate, was what it sounded like. But when one was actually with her, looking into her face, it was almost impossible not to take her seriously.

He arrived home to find the table already set for dinner. Kissing his wife on both cheeks, he said:

"It's been such a lovely day. I hope you managed to get out."

"I did some shopping."

And then he said something that surprised her.

"Tell me, have you ever sat on a bench in a public park?"

She was taken aback by the question. After a moment's reflection she said:

"I suppose I must have, when I was too early for a dental appointment, for instance."

"I had a visitor this evening who spends almost every afternoon sitting on a bench in the Tuileries."

"There are lots of people like that."

"Have you ever talked with any of them?"

"On one occasion, at least. The mother of a little girl asked me to keep an eye on her while she got something from a shop just across the square."

Here, too, a window was open. They had several kinds of cold cuts and a salad with mayonnaise. It might have been the height of summer.

"How about a short walk?"

There was still a rosy glow in the sky from the setting sun, and it was quiet on the Boulevard Richard-Lenoir. Here and there they could see people looking down into the street, their elbows resting on the window sills.

They enjoyed walking for its own sake. It was pleasant to be together, though they had nothing much to say to one another. Together they watched the people crossing the streets, together they looked at the window displays in the shops, and occasionally one or the other would make a remark. They went as far as the Bastille and came back along the Boulevard Beaumarchais.

"A very strange old lady came to see me this evening,

though actually it was Lapointe who interviewed her. I didn't see her until later, when she stopped me in the street as I was leaving.

"From the story she tells you'd think she was mad, or at least a bit touched."

"What's her trouble?"

"Nothing, really. It's just that she says that sometimes, when she's been out, she comes back to find some of her things slightly out of place."

"Does she have a cat?"

"That was the first thing Lapointe asked her. She doesn't have any pets. She lives above a shop that sells birds, and she can hear them singing all day long, which she says is company enough for her."

"Do you think there's any truth in it?"

"When she was actually there, looking up at me, yes, I did. She's got wonderfully clear gray eyes, full of kindliness and honesty, utterly without guile, at any rate. She's been widowed twelve years. She lives alone. Except for a niece whom she hardly ever sees, she has no one in the world.

"Every morning she goes out to the local shops, in a white hat and gloves. She spends most of her afternoons sitting on a bench in the Tuileries. She doesn't complain, she's never bored, and loneliness doesn't seem to worry her."

"That's true of a lot of old people, you know."

"I guess you're right, but there's something a little different about her, though I can't quite put my finger on it."

It was dark by the time they got home, and much cooler. They went to bed early, and next morning, since it was another lovely day, Maigret decided to walk to work.

As usual, there was a formidable pile of letters for him. He just had time to glance through them and have a word with his inspectors before the Director's daily briefing. There was nothing very important on hand.

He spent the morning clearing up a few routine matters and then decided, on the spur of the moment, to have lunch at the Brasserie Dauphine. He called his wife to tell her he would not be home for lunch. He had intended, after he had eaten, to call on the old lady at the Quai de la Mégisserie and was prevented from doing so only by the merest chance. He ran into an old colleague, whom he had not seen since his retirement, and they lingered for a quarter of an hour or more, chatting in the sunshine.

Twice that afternoon he thought again of going to see the old lady, whom the inspectors had already nicknamed "Maigret's old madwoman," but each time, he found some excuse for putting it off, telling himself that tomorrow would do just as well.

If the newspapers were ever to get hold of the tale of the wandering ornaments, he would be the laughingstock of Paris.

That evening they stayed in and watched television. Next morning he overslept and had to go to work by bus. A few minutes before noon, the Divisional Superintendent of the 1st *Arrondissement* called him.

"Something has happened here that I think may be of interest to your people. The concierge of the apartment house tells me that one of your inspectors, a young fellow, very handsome, called to see her the other day."

He had a sudden foreboding.

"At the Quai de la Mégisserie?"

"Yes."

"Is she dead?"

"Yes."

"Are you calling from the apartment?"

"I'm downstairs in the bird shop. There's no telephone up there."

"I'm on my way."

He put his head around the door of the inspectors' duty room and said to Lapointe:

"Come with me."

"Anything wrong, Chief?"

"As far as you and I are concerned, yes, very wrong. It's the old lady."

"The one with the gray eyes and the white hat?"

"Yes. She's dead."

"Murdered?"

"I presume so. Why else would the Superintendent have thought fit to get in touch with me?"

They didn't bother with a car. It was quicker to walk. Superintendent Jenton, well known to Maigret, was standing on the edge of the sidewalk, next to a parrot chained to its perch.

"Did you know her?"

"I saw her only once. I'd promised to come to see her as soon as I could. Yesterday, I nearly did."

Would it have made any difference if he had?

"Is there anyone up there?"

"One of my men, and Doctor Forniaux has just arrived."

"How did she die?"

"I don't know yet. At about half past ten this morning, one of the fourth-floor tenants noticed that her door was ajar. She didn't think anything of it and went out to do her shopping. When she got back at eleven and saw it was still open, she called out:

" 'Madame Antoine! . . . Madame Antoine! . . . Are you there?'

"When there was no answer, she went into the apartment and nearly tripped over the body."

"Was it on the floor?"

"Yes. In the living room. The neighbor had the good sense to call us at once."

Maigret went slowly up the stairs. His expression was grim.

"How was she dressed?"

"She must have been out earlier. She was still wearing her white hat and gloves."

"Any visible injuries?"

"None that I could see. The concierge told me that one of your men was here two days ago, asking questions about the old lady, so, of course, I called you at once."

Doctor Forniaux, who was kneeling on the floor, stood up as the three men came into the room.

They shook hands.

"Can you tell us the cause of death?"

"Suffocation."

"Do you mean she was strangled?"

"No. Some sort of cloth—a towel, perhaps, or even a handkerchief—was held over her nose and mouth until she stopped breathing."

"Are you sure?"

"I'll be able to tell you for certain after the autopsy."

The window was wide open, and they could hear the birds twittering in the shop below.

"When did she die?"

"Sometime yesterday. Late afternoon or early evening."

In death, the old woman seemed even tinier than she had when she was alive. Lying there, so small, with one leg bent at an awkward angle, she looked like a disjointed puppet.

The doctor had closed her eyes. Her face and hands seemed carved in ivory.

"How long before the killer could be sure she was dead, would you say?"

"It's hard to tell, especially with a woman of her age. Five minutes perhaps, a little more, a little less . . ."

"Lapointe, call up Public Prosecutions and the Laboratory. Tell Moers to send his men right away."

"Unless there's something else I can do for you," said the Police Doctor, "I'll be on my way. I'll arrange for the hearse to take her to the Forensic Laboratory as soon as you've finished with her."

A small crowd was beginning to gather outside the building. The Divisional Superintendent sent his man down to speak to them.

"Get them moving. This isn't a public entertainment."

Murder was scarcely a new experience for either of them, but they were nonetheless deeply affected. She was so very old and—what made it seem worse—there was not even a mark on her.

Then there was the atmosphere of the place, recalling the Edwardian, if not the Victorian, era. The furniture was of solid mahogany, massive pieces, all beautifully polished to a high gloss. The chairs, of the kind still to be found in country drawing rooms, were covered in crimson plush. There were a great many knickknacks and masses of photographs hanging on every wall, against a background of flowered paper.

"All we can do now is wait for the Deputy Public Prosecutor."

"He won't be long. They'll send the first available one. He'll arrive with his clerk, take a quick look around, and that will be that."

This, indeed, was a fair description of what usually happened as a prelude to the arrival of the Forensic technicians, with all their cumbersome apparatus.

The door swung open without a sound. Maigret gave a start. A little girl sidled in, probably a neighbor's child, curious to see what all the comings and goings were about.

"Do you come here often?"

"No, I've never been here before."

"Where do you live?"

"Just across the landing."

"Did you know Madame Antoine?"

"I used to see her sometimes on the stairs."

"Did she ever talk to you?"

"She always smiled at me."

"Did she ever give you anything, candy or chocolates?"

"No."

"Where's your mother?"

"In the kitchen."

"Take me to her, will you?"

He turned to the Superintendent.

"Excuse me for a moment. I'd be grateful if you'd let me know when the Deputy gets here."

It was an old building. The walls were bulging in places, and there were gaps between the floorboards.

"There's a man to see you, Mommy."

25

The woman came out of the kitchen, wiping her hands on her apron. Her arms, just below the elbow, were still spattered with soapsuds.

"I'm Chief Superintendent Maigret. I just happened to be in the apartment across the landing when your daughter walked in. Was it you who found the body?"

"What body? Go to your room, Lucette."

"Your neighbor, opposite."

"So she's dead? I always said it was bound to happen sooner or later. A woman of her age shouldn't live alone. No doubt she was taken bad, and didn't have the strength to call for help."

"She was murdered."

"I never heard a thing! But then, of course, with all the noise of the traffic ..."

"There was no shooting, and it happened not this morning, but yesterday afternoon or evening."

"Poor woman! She was a bit too high and mighty for my taste, but I didn't have anything against her."

"Were you on friendly terms with her?"

"I doubt if we exchanged a dozen words in all the seven years I've lived here."

"Do you know anything about her personal life?"

"I often used to see her go out in the morning. She wore a black hat in winter and a white one in summer, and she never went out without her gloves, even around the corner to the shops. Well, live and let live, I always say."

"Did she ever have visitors?"

"Not that I know of. No, wait, come to think of it, she did have one, a woman, rather on the heavy side, and a bit mannish. I saw her two or three times ringing the door-bell."

"Was this during the day?"

"Usually in the evening. Soon after dinner."

"Have you noticed any unusual comings and goings in the building recently?"

"There are always people milling around. The concierge hardly ever leaves the lodge, there, across the yard. She takes no interest at all in the tenants."

The little girl had sidled back noiselessly into the room. The woman turned to her.

"Didn't you hear what I said? Go straight back to your room."

"You'll probably be seeing me again. I'll have to speak with all the tenants."

"I suppose you don't have any idea who did it?"

"None."

"Who found her?"

"Someone from the fourth floor. She noticed on her way out that the door was ajar, and when she came back and found it still open, she called out and then went in."

"I can guess who that was."

"Why do you say that?"

"It must be old Mother Rochin. She's the nosiest woman in the building."

They could hear footsteps and voices outside on the landing. The men from the Public Prosecutor's Office had arrived. Maigret went across to join them.

"This way," he said. "Doctor Forniaux has been here, but he has a great many calls this morning, so he couldn't wait."

The Deputy Public Prosecutor was a tall young man, distinguished-looking and strikingly well dressed. He looked around him in some surprise, as though he had never seen anything quite like it. Then he stood for a moment staring down at the crumpled little gray figure on the carpet.

"How did she die?"

"She was suffocated."

"She couldn't have put up much of a fight, that's for sure."

Judge Libart arrived a few minutes later. He, too, looked around the apartment with interest.

"It's just like an old movie set," he remarked.

By this time Lapointe had returned. He and Maigret exchanged glances. While neither of them actually shuddered, their feelings were plain enough.

Chapter 2

"Maybe I'd better send along two or three men to keep the sightseers on the move," suggested the Divisional Superintendent.

Already the residents were pouring out of their apartments and gathering on the landing and staircase. The Deputy and his clerk did not take long, and the stretcher bearers from the Forensic Laboratory carried the corpse away.

Lapointe, glancing at Maigret, noted that he was looking unusually pale and grave. It was only two days since he had first set eyes on the dead woman. Up to that time, he had never even heard of her. Yet, in her distress—real or imagined—it was to him that she had turned for help. She had put her trust in him. She had sought a personal interview and, failing that, had stopped him in the street. He could still see her looking up at him, her eyes glowing with hero worship.

He had thought her mad, or at least not perfectly sane. And yet, all the while, there had been that little nagging doubt at the back of his mind. And so he had promised to go to see her. And probably would have done so, this very afternoon.

It was too late now. Her fears had been well justified. She had indeed been killed.

"See that they go over every inch of every room for fingerprints. Make sure they don't miss anything, not even the least likely surfaces."

There was a sudden commotion on the landing. He opened the front door. At least a dozen reporters and cameramen were crowding around the door, with a solitary policeman struggling to hold them back.

A microphone was pushed toward his face.

"Can you give us a statement, Chief Superintendent?"

"Not at the moment, gentlemen, I'm afraid. You might say that the inquiry hasn't really started yet."

"Who was she?"

"An old lady."

"Madame Antoine de Caramé. That much we got from the concierge. What's more, she says that one of your men was here earlier in the week, asking questions about her. What was that for? Did you have any reason to think she was in danger?"

"All I can say now is that I'm as much in the dark as you are."

"Is it true that she lived alone and never had any visitors?"

"As far as we know, that's correct, except for a niece—I don't know her name—who used to come to see her from time to time. She's a masseuse and lives quite near here, just across the river, not far from the Pont-Neuf."

A brief statement to this effect had already been broadcast and would also be featured in the afternoon editions of the newspapers. As a result, no doubt the niece would in due course come forward.

"May we go in to take pictures?"

"Not yet. The men from Criminal Records haven't finished. For the time being, I'd be obliged if you would leave the landing and staircase clear."

"We'll wait downstairs in the courtyard."

Maigret closed the door. He had not yet had time to inspect the apartment. Overlooking the street was the living room, where Madame Antoine had been attacked, no doubt on returning from her daily outing to the Tuileries.

Had she been right in suspecting that someone was entering the apartment while she was out? It seemed more than likely. If so, there was something here that the intruder very badly wanted. But what could it possibly be?

She must have gotten home earlier than usual and surprised the intruder, who then put her out of the way. That seemed to suggest that he was someone she recognized. If not, he could easily have fled. Had he had no other choice but to kill her?

"Any fingerprints?"

"None but the old lady's so far. Oh, and the Police Doctor's on the table in the living room. I'd know them anywhere."

There were two windows in the living room, which was low-ceilinged like the rest of the apartment. A door led into the dining room. Both rooms were quaintly old-fashioned, as old-fashioned as Madame Antoine herself. On a pedestal table in the corner stood an enormous green plant in an earthenware pot, which was swathed in drapery.

Everything was spotlessly clean, and there was not a thing out of place.

There was only one window in the dining room, and, facing it, a door that led into the kitchen. The loaf in the breadbox was still fresh. Maigret opened the refrigerator. It contained, neatly wrapped in pieces of wax paper, a slice of ham and half a veal cutlet. There were also a head of lettuce and a half bottle of milk.

There was only one other room, the bedroom. Like the kitchen, it looked out onto the courtyard. The bedroom furniture, which included a massive mirror-fronted wardrobe and an imposing bed, was of walnut. The floorboards were covered by a faded, threadbare carpet, vaguely oriental in design.

There was an indefinable air of dignity about the whole place. He would have to come back later, after lunch probably, to examine the old lady's possessions one by one, including the contents of the cupboards and drawers.

"We're through now, Chief."

The police photographers were dismantling and removing their cameras. No fingerprints had been found, other than those of the old lady herself.

Maigret instructed the officer at the door to admit no one except the inspector, whom he would be sending up in a moment. He went slowly down the dark staircase, with its worn treads and banister polished to a high gloss by two or three hundred years of use.

In the courtyard, the newspapermen were bombarding the concierge with questions, and getting short shrift for their pains. Lapointe, unusually silent, followed Maigret downstairs. He, too, was much shaken. He had a mental picture of Madame Antoine as he had seen her in the little office where he had interviewed her and formed the impression that she was not quite right in the head.

The owner of the birds—Monsieur Caille, presumably, since that was the name painted over his shop—wearing long, gray denim overalls, was standing on the sidewalk beside a row of cages.

"I wonder if I might use your telephone?"

"Go right ahead, Chief Superintendent."

He gave a knowing smile, very pleased with himself for having recognized Maigret. The telephone was at the back of the shop, where, in addition to more birds in cages, there were several tanks full of goldfish. An old man, also in gray overalls, was engaged in feeding the fish.

"Hello! . . . Lucas? . . . I'll be needing another man here. . . . Quai de la Mégisserie . . . Eight B . . . Janvier? . . . Fine . . . Tell him to go straight up to the apartment and not to let anyone else in. . . . And I'd be obliged if you'd call my wife and tell her I won't be home for lunch. . . ."

He put down the receiver and returned to the pet-shop owner.

"Have you lived here long?"

"Ever since I was ten years old. My father owned the shop before me."

"So you've known Madame Antoine ever since she moved in?"

"Yes, it must be forty years. That was in the time of her first husband, Monsieur de Caramé. A fine-looking man, he was. Impressive. He was very high up in local govern-

33

ment, and whenever there was a do at City Hall, he always gave us complimentary tickets."

"Did they do much entertaining in those early days?"

"There were two or three married couples who were close friends of theirs. They used to get together for a game of cards about once a week."

"What was Madame Antoine like?"

"She was a dear little thing. Very pretty. It's strange how things turn out, though. She was so frail and delicate you'd never have thought she'd make old bones. He, on the other hand, was strongly built and, as far as I know, never had a day's illness. He enjoyed the good things of life. Yet he was the one who died suddenly in his office, when he was in the prime of life, while his wife lived on—until yesterday."

"And she remarried soon after?"

"Oh, no. She was alone for the best part of ten years. Then she met Monsieur Antoine somewhere or other and eventually married him. I have nothing to say against him. He was a thoroughly decent fellow, but, compared with her first husband, he lacked distinction.

"He worked in the Hôtel de Ville department store. He was head of one of the departments, I believe. He was a widower. You've probably seen his little workshop up there. He loved nothing better than to be puttering around in there. He never said much beyond passing the time of day. They hardly ever went out.

"He had a car and used to take his wife for a drive in the country on Sundays. In the summer, they always went on vacation to a place somewhere near Étretat."

"Were any of the other tenants friends of theirs?"

"I guess I must be the only one left. The others have all

died off in the course of the years, and new people have moved in to take their place. I never see any of the old faces nowadays."

"There's Monsieur Crispin, don't forget, Father," interpolated the son, who was standing in the doorway.

"True enough, but since we never see him around now, it's hard to remember that he's still alive. He's paralyzed—has been for the past five years. He has a couple of rooms on the top floor, and the concierge takes his meals up to him and cleans the place for him."

"Was he friendly with the Antoines?"

"Let me think. At my age, you tend to lose track of time. He moved in a little while before Madame Antoine. So Monsieur de Caramé must have been still alive. But I don't think they were on visiting terms at that time. It was only later, when Madame de Caramé married Monsieur Antoine, that they became friends. He was in business, too, you see—haberdashery, I think. He worked in a shop on the Rue du Sentier."

"I'm much obliged to you, Monsieur Caille."

Janvier was waiting for him in the front hall.

"Did you have something to eat?"

"A snack, but what about you?"

"Lapointe and I are just off to lunch. I want you to go up and wait for us in the apartment. It's on the second floor. Don't touch anything, anything at all, however insignificant. You'll find out why later. Oh! There's just one person you'll have to let in if she turns up, and that's the niece."

Ten minutes later Maigret and Lapointe were seated at a table in the Brasserie Dauphine.

"An apéritif?" suggested the proprietor.

"No, bring us a carafe of Beaujolais right away. What have you got on the menu today?"

"*Andouillettes*. They arrived fresh from Auvergne this morning."

Maigret ordered herring fillet as a first course, to be followed by the *andouillettes*.

"What do you think?" asked Maigret, a little uncomfortably.

Lapointe was at a loss as to what to say.

"It never entered my head that she was telling the truth. I could have sworn that she was just imagining things, the way old people so often do."

"She's dead."

"And if the door hadn't been left ajar, it might have been days before anyone found her. The murderer must have been someone she knew, otherwise he wouldn't have had to kill her."

"I wonder what it was he was looking for."

"When we know that—if we ever do—the case will be virtually solved. Next we shall be going over the apartment inch by inch. There must be something there that the murderer very much wanted to find. He searched the place several times without success, so it's probably well hidden or not immediately recognizable."

"What if he's already found what he was looking for?"

"In that case, there's not much hope of catching him. All the other tenants will have to be questioned. How many floors are there in the building?"

"Six, excluding the attic."

"And there are at least two apartments on every floor...."

The Beaujolais could not have been better, and the *andouillettes,* served with chips, were delicious.

"There's one thing that puzzles me. Madame Antoine was eighty-six. She'd been a widow for twelve years or more. Why wait until now to start searching her apartment? Surely that must mean that whatever it is that the intruder was looking for had only recently come into the old lady's possession."

"If that's the case, she would have known what it was. But, if I'm not mistaken, she told you that she hadn't the least idea what it was all about."

"She seemed just as puzzled as we were."

"There was no mystery about either of her husbands. Quite the contrary. Both were typical middle-class Frenchmen, except that one was rather better-looking than the other."

Maigret beckoned the proprietor.

"Two coffees, Léon."

The sun was still shining in a cloudless blue sky. The Quais were crowded with tourists, with cameras slung around their necks.

The two men made their way back to the Quai de la Mégisserie. All but one of the reporters had left, and he was pacing restlessly up and down the courtyard.

"I don't suppose there's anything you can tell me?" he muttered, somewhat sourly.

"Nothing now."

"There's a woman up there. She arrived about ten minutes ago, but she wouldn't give her name."

It was not long before Maigret and Lapointe were making her acquaintance. She was a heavily built woman of somewhat mannish appearance, aged about forty-five to fifty. She was seated in one of the armchairs in the living room.

Janvier, apparently, had not attempted to engage her in conversation.

"Are you Chief Superintendent Maigret?"

"Yes, and these two gentlemen are Inspectors Janvier and Lapointe."

"I am Angèle Louette."

"Madame?"

"No, I'm not married, though I have a son twenty-five years old. I'm not ashamed of it. Quite the contrary."

"You are Madame Antoine's niece, I take it?"

"She and my mother were sisters. She was the elder, although my mother was the first to go. She's been dead more than ten years now."

"Does your son live with you?"

"No, I'm by myself. I have a small apartment on the Rue Saint-André-des-Arts."

"And your son?"

"He moves around a good deal. I believe he's now on the Riviera. He's a musician."

"When did you last see your aunt?"

"About three weeks ago."

"Did you visit her often?"

"About once a month. Sometimes once in two months."

"Did you get along well with her?"

"We didn't quarrel."

"Which means . . ."

"We were never at all close. My aunt was a mistrustful old woman. I'm sure she believed I came to see her only to keep on good terms with her, in the hope of inheriting her money."

"Did she have anything to leave?"

"She must have had savings, but I don't think they amounted to much."

"Do you know if she had a bank account?"

"If so, she never told me. She was always insisting that I see to it that she was buried beside her first husband in Montparnasse Cemetery. She has a plot there.

"If you want my opinion, I think she remarried only for the sake of company. She was still young. I don't know where she met my Uncle Antoine. The first I heard of it was one day when she announced, out of the blue, that she was getting married again and asked me to be a witness. . . ."

Maigret was taking in every word, having motioned to Lapointe, who had got out his shorthand pad, that he did not wish him to take notes. She was the kind of woman who would probably shut up like a clam if subjected to an official interrogation.

"Tell me, Mademoiselle Louette, do you know of any reason why your aunt should have been in fear of her life?"

"None at all."

"Did she tell you that she had found traces of a mysterious intruder in the apartment?"

"No, never."

"Did she ever call or come to see you?"

"No. I always came to see her. Just from time to time, you know, to make sure she was all right, and to find out if there was anything she needed. It worried me that she lived by herself. Anything might have happened to her, and not a soul would have known."

"Did she ever consider having a cleaning woman to help with the housework?"

"She could well have afforded it, on her two widow's pensions. I begged her to get someone to live in, but she wouldn't hear even of a cleaning woman. You can see how she kept the apartment. Not a speck of dust anywhere."

"You are a masseuse, I believe."

"Yes, my time is fully occupied. I have nothing to complain of."

"Tell me about your son's father."

"He left me when my son was born. I wasn't sorry to see him go. He wasn't the man I thought he was. I lost my head over him, as they say. I've no idea what's become of him, and I don't think I'd recognize him now if I met him in the street."

"I take it, then, that your son bears your name and has 'father unknown' stamped on his birth certificate?"

"Yes. His name is Émile Louette. But since he took up the guitar and became a night-club entertainer, he's become known, for professional purposes, as Billy Louette."

"Are you and he on good terms?"

"He comes to see me occasionally, usually when he's short of money. He lives like a gypsy, but he's a good kid, all the same."

"Did he ever come to see his aunt?"

"I used to bring him with me when he was a child. The last time was when he was fifteen or sixteen, I think. As far as I know, he's never seen her since."

"Do you think he might have come to her for money, the way he came to you?"

"He wouldn't do a thing like that. I'm his mother, so that's different, but he would never ask anyone else. He's too proud."

"Do you know your way around this apartment?"

"Pretty well."

"Where did your aunt spend most of her time?"

"Here, in this very armchair, drawn up close to the window."

"How did she keep herself busy?"

"First of all, she had the housework to do. Then she'd go out to do her shopping. When she got back, she'd cook herself a meal. She wasn't the sort to settle for a slice of cold meat eaten off a corner of the kitchen table. In spite of the fact that she lived alone, she took her meals in the dining room, and the table was always properly set, with a clean cloth."

"Did she go out much?"

"On fine days she liked to go and sit on a bench in the Tuileries."

"Did she read a lot?"

"No. She had weak eyesight, and it tired her to read for any length of time. She enjoyed watching the people out for a stroll, and the children playing among the trees. She almost always wore a rather sad little smile. I suppose she lived in the past a good deal."

"Did she ever confide in you?"

"What could she possibly have had to tell me? Her life was an open book."

"Didn't she have any friends?"

"All her old friends had died, and she didn't feel like

making new ones; and that was why she moved away from the bench she had always sat on. I've just remembered."

"How long ago was this?"

"Toward the end of last summer. For years she'd always sat on the same bench in the Tuileries Gardens. One day she was approached by a woman of about her own age, who asked if she might share the bench with her. Presumably she said yes. Anyone is at liberty to sit down on a park bench. At any rate, this woman tried to strike up an acquaintance with her from the very first day. She told her that she was of Russian origin, and that she had been, in her day, a famous ballerina.

"Next day she was there again and spent an hour regaling my aunt with tales of her former glory. She had lived in Nice for years, and she went on and on about the awful Paris weather.

"My aunt wasn't given to idle chatter as a rule.

" 'I had become so attached to that bench!' she said, with a sigh.

" 'Not only was I forced to move away from it, but I had to go right to the other side of the Gardens, otherwise she'd have found me, and I would never have got away from her.' "

"Did this Russian woman ever visit her here?"

"Not that I know of. My aunt being what she was, I'm pretty sure she never got the chance."

"You can't throw any light on the identity of the murderer, I suppose?"

"I'm afraid not, Chief Superintendent. What should I do about the funeral arrangements?"

"You'd better let me have your telephone number. I'll

be in touch. By the way, do you happen to have a recent photograph of your aunt?"

"Only one taken by my Uncle Antoine about twelve years ago. I'd be grateful if you'd call me in the evening, since I'm at work most of the day."

It was the rule to have a police officer assigned to keep watch at the entrance.

"What do you make of her, Chief?"

"She seems ready enough to talk. Rather a bossy woman, I'd say."

Janvier looked about him in astonishment.

"Is it all like this?"

"Yes. The bedroom, if anything, is even more Old-World. Lapointe, you know the layout of the building, more or less. I want you to call at all the apartments. Find out which of the tenants knew the old lady by sight, and whether any of them were at all friendly with her. Also, of course, whether they ever saw anyone entering or leaving the apartment."

The only concession to the twentieth century was the television set in the living room. It stood in a corner, facing an armchair upholstered in flowered chintz.

"Now," said Maigret to Janvier, "we're going to go over the apartment inch by inch, recording the exact position of everything in it. It's because she found some of her things very slightly displaced that she first got alarmed."

The shrunken floorboards, with gaps between, were covered not with a carpet but with scattered rugs, on one of which stood a round tripod table covered with a lace cloth.

They moved the table and took up the rug, to satisfy themselves that nothing was hidden under it. Having done so, they returned the table to its original position and carefully put back the knickknacks: a large seashell with "Dieppe" carved on it, an earthenware planter, and a fake bronze statuette of a schoolboy in a sailor suit with a satchel on his back.

The mantelpiece was covered with photographs: photographs of two men, the two husbands of the old lady, who, toward the end, it seemed, had almost forgotten which was which. One of them—round-faced, plump, and clean-shaven—had struck a dignified stance before the camera. He, no doubt, was the one who had been a senior official at City Hall.

The other, somewhat less impressive, had a graying mustache. Men like him were to be seen in the thousands every day on the buses and the *métro*. He looked more like a clerk or a cashier than the manager or buyer of a large store, which was what he had actually been. He was smiling in the photograph, a cheerful smile. He had been content with his lot.

"By the way, Janvier, how did the niece get in? Did she have a key?"

"No, she rang the bell, and I let her in."

"This drawer is locked. The key must be around somewhere."

First he searched through the contents of the old lady's handbag, the white leather handbag she must only recently have got out of her wardrobe, for use in the spring and summer. There was no lipstick; just a powder compact—the powder had a bluish tinge—and a handkerchief embroidered with the initial *L*. Madame Antoine's Christian name, as the two men were soon to find out, had been Léontine.

No cigarettes. Obviously she didn't smoke. A small bag of violet-scented candies from a shop on the Rue de Rivoli. The candies must have been there for some time, since they were all stuck together.

"Here are the keys."

He had been almost sure that he would find her keys in the handbag that went everywhere with her. There were three keys for furniture, a key to one of the rooms, and the front-door key.

"She opened the door and put the keys back in her bag before coming in. Otherwise, they would have been left in the lock, or we would have found them on the floor. She must barely have had time to put her bag down on the chair before she was attacked."

Maigret was not so much addressing Janvier as thinking aloud. He could not get rid of a nagging sense of uneasiness. Yet, even if he had been to see the old lady, would it have made that much difference? He would not have been able to find enough evidence to justify keeping a twenty-four-hour watch on the apartment. And the murderer, unaware of his visit, would still have acted as he did.

He tried the smaller keys, one after the other, and finally succeeded in opening the locked drawer of the chest.

It was full of papers and photographs. On the right-hand side lay a Post Office Savings book in the name of Léontine Antoine, Quai de la Mégisserie, recording deposits amounting to ten thousand francs; nothing but deposits, not a single withdrawal. She had been paying money into the account for twenty-five years, which was why the name "Caramé" could still be read, with a line through it, below the name "Antoine."

Twenty-five years of thrift. Shopping in the morning. An hour or so on a park bench in the afternoon. Perhaps an occasional visit to a movie when the weather was bad. There was also a Savings Bank book, recording a total of twenty-three thousand two hundred francs. A few days before Christmas in the previous year, there had been a withdrawal of two thousand five hundred francs.

"What does that suggest to you?"

Janvier shook his head.

"The television set. I'll bet you anything that's where the two thousand five hundred francs went. In other words, she decided to give herself a treat for Christmas."

The only other recorded withdrawal was twelve years old and, no doubt, represented the cost of her second husband's funeral.

There were numerous postcards, most of them signed "Jean." They bore the postmarks of various towns and cities in France, Belgium, and Switzerland. The sender must have been attending conferences in these places. All the cards bore the same message: "Much love, Jean," in a distinguished, curved hand. "Jean" was Caramé. Antoine, apparently, had seldom been away by himself. There was not a single card from him. But there were innumerable photographs both of him alone and of him and his wife. The camera with which they had been taken, a rather sophisticated one, was also in the same drawer. Monsieur and Madame Antoine, it seemed, had gone to a different place each year for their vacation. Apparently, they had been great travelers. They had visited Quimper, La Baule,

Arcachon, and Biarritz. They had toured the Massif Central and spent summers on the Riviera.

The photographs had been taken at different times; in some the couple appeared older than in others. It would have been a simple matter to arrange them in chronological order.

There were a few letters, mostly from Angèle Louette, the niece who was a masseuse. These, too, came from towns outside Paris.

"Émile and I are thoroughly enjoying our vacation. Émile is growing up fast. He spends all day rolling over and over in the sand. . . ."

There was just one photograph of the boy, Émile, who was now calling himself Billy. It was taken when he was fifteen. He was looking straight in front of him, with an expression that spelled defiance of the whole world.

"No secrets. No surprises," sighed Maigret.

In the drawer of a little table they found nothing but some pencils, a pen, an eraser, and a few sheets of plain writing paper. Léontine had probably written few letters recently. Who was left for her to write to?

She had outlived most of her contemporaries. Her niece and great-nephew were her only remaining relatives, and the boy scarcely counted. There was no trace of him among her things, except for that one photograph and the references in his mother's letter.

While sorting through the kitchen utensils, Maigret came upon several gadgets that were unfamiliar to him, and that did not look as though they were mass-produced. There was, for instance, a can opener of highly sophisticated design, as well as a simple but ingenious potato peeler.

It was not until he discovered the little cubbyhole across the way that he understood the significance of these appliances. The key to the door was on Madame Antoine's key ring. It opened on to a tiny annex, quite separate from the apartment itself, which was lit by a skylight overlooking the courtyard. This annex was furnished with a workbench and a wide selection of tools, hanging neatly from hooks all around the walls.

This, then, was where Monsieur Antoine had pursued his hobby. On a shelf in one corner stood a pile of technical journals, and there was a drawer full of notebooks filled with technical drawings of all kinds, including a drawing of the potato peeler.

There must be thousands of people like him all over Paris, thought Maigret, thousands of couples like the Antoines, living modest, tidy, well-organized lives. There was only one discordant note: the murder of the tiny old woman with the marvelously clear gray eyes.

"There's still the bedroom and the cupboards."

The entire contents of the wardrobe consisted of a Persian-lamb coat, another of black wool, two winter dresses, one of which was mauve, and three or four summer dresses.

No men's clothes. After the death of her second husband she must have given away his things, unless she had stored them somewhere else, possibly in the attic. He must find out from the concierge.

Everything was very clean and tidy, and all the drawers were lined with white paper.

But the lining paper of the bedside-table drawer, which, incidentally, was empty, was discolored by a large oil or grease stain.

Maigret, intrigued, took the paper out of the drawer and held it up to his nose. He called Janvier over, to see what he could make of it.

"What do you think this is?"

"Grease."

"Yes, but not just any sort of grease. It's gun grease. The old lady must have kept a revolver or an automatic in this drawer."

"Where is it now?"

"Not in the apartment, that's for sure. We've searched every inch, and we haven't found it. Even so, it looks quite fresh to me. Do you suppose the old woman's killer . . . ?"

It seemed highly unlikely that the murderer, whether man or woman, would have spent time looking for the revolver before making his or her getaway.

This grease stain, which he had not discovered until the very end of his search, was a complication that he had not anticipated.

Had the old woman actually gone to the length of buying a gun to defend herself? It seemed unlikely. From what Maigret had seen of her, she was hardly the sort to look upon firearms with anything but alarm. Moreover, he simply could not imagine her going into a gunsmith's, asking for a pistol, and trudging down to the basement for a few practice shots.

And yet, when all was said and done, why not? Hadn't he been struck by her extraordinary vitality? Frail she certainly had been, with her delicate wrists no thicker than a child's, yet her apartment was as well cared for as any he could think of, even better perhaps.

"It must have belonged to one of her husbands."

"But, then, where has it gone? See that this paper is handed in to the Lab for analysis, though I'm quite sure in my own mind what the answer will be."

A bell rang, and Maigret instinctively looked around for the telephone.

"It's the front door," said Janvier.

He went to open it. It was Lapointe, looking absolutely worn out.

"Have you spoken to all the tenants?"

"All except those who were out. The worst of it is, I could hardly get a word in with any of them. It was nothing but questions, questions, questions! How did she die? What was the murder weapon? How come that no one had heard a shot?"

"Go on."

"The apartment immediately above is occupied by an elderly bachelor of about sixty. Apparently, he's quite a well-known historian. I saw some of his books on his library shelves. He seldom goes out. He lives alone with his little dog. He has a housekeeper who comes in daily to clean the apartment and cook his meals. I say a housekeeper because that's how he described her. I saw her for myself. She's known as Mademoiselle Élise, and she's full of her own importance.

"It's almost as old-fashioned as this apartment, except that it's furnished in better taste. In passing he said:

" 'If only she hadn't bought that wretched television set! She had it on almost every night until eleven. And I'm up every morning at six, to get in my regular walk before breakfast.' "

Lapointe went on:

"They never exchanged a word in all the twenty years

he's been living here. When they met on the stairs, they merely nodded. He remembers the husband, because he was noisy, too. Apparently he had a workshop and a regular armory of tools, and he would be sawing, hammering, filing, and heaven knows what else until all hours."

"What about the apartment opposite?"

"There was no one at home. I went down to the concierge to inquire about them. They're youngish people, apparently. He's a film technician, some sort of sound engineer, and his wife works in the cutting room. They usually eat out and get home very late. They're late risers, too, and they don't leave for work until noon."

"And the fourth floor?"

Lapointe glanced at his notes.

"Some people called Lapin. There was no one in but the grandmother and the baby. The wife works in a men's-wear shop on the Rue de Rivoli, and the husband is an insurance salesman. He's away a lot."

"What about the apartment opposite?"

"I'll come to them in a minute. I spoke to the grand-mother, and she said:

" 'No, young man, I did not know her. That woman was too smart, if you ask me. Look at the way she behaved with those two husbands of hers. I'm a widow myself, but did I go out looking for another husband? You wouldn't catch me setting up house with another man, in the same apartment, with the same furniture.' "

Once again Lapointe consulted his notes.

"Father Raymond. I don't know which order he belongs to. He's very old and scarcely ever sets foot outside his apartment.

"He didn't even know of the existence of Léontine Antoine, formerly Léontine de Caramé. . . .

"On the floor above that, there's an empty apartment, rented to people who will be moving in in a fortnight. The workmen are there now, redecorating. The new tenants are a couple of about forty, with two children at the *lycée.*

"I interviewed the old man the concierge helps out. He's confined to a wheel chair, and you should just see how he gets around in it! I was expecting to see a querulous old dodderer, but not a bit of it; he's as chirpy as a cricket:

" 'Not really!' he exclaimed. 'So she's actually gone and got herself murdered! I've been here fifty years or more, and nothing of any interest has ever happened before. And now we have a murder of our very own! Do you know who did it? I don't suppose it could possibly be a crime of passion, do you?' "

Lapointe went on:

"It was really comical. He was enjoying himself immensely. If it had been physically possible, he would have asked permission to visit the scene of the crime.

"The woman opposite is a Madame Blanche. She's about sixty and works as a cashier in a brasserie. I didn't see her, since she doesn't get in before midnight."

It was a tight little world that all these people lived in side by side, and yet the murder of the old lady on the second floor had caused scarcely a ripple.

"How was she killed?"

"Who did it?"

"Why didn't she call out?"

Most of these people knew one another by sight and would nod in passing, without exchanging a word. A lot of little private cells, with the doors shut tight.

"I want you to stay here until I send someone to relieve you," Maigret said to Janvier.

"It may seem farfetched, but I have a notion that the man or woman who searched this apartment before may well do so again."

"Send Torrence, if you can spare him. He's crazy about television."

Maigret took the grease-stained lining paper with him. As soon as he got back to the Quai des Orfèvres, he went straight up to Moers in his domain in the attic.

"I want this stain analyzed."

Moers sniffed at it, nodded to Maigret as if to assure him that this was no problem, and went over to one of the many technicians at work in the huge laboratory under the sloping roof of the building.

"It's as I thought, gun grease."

"I'll need an official report. It's the only clue we've got so far. Is it an old stain, would you say?"

"My man says that will take a little time to establish."

"Thanks. Send down the result when you have it."

He returned to his office, stopping off at the inspectors' duty room on the way. Lapointe was writing his report, with his notebook open beside him. Torrence was also there.

"Well, Torrence, are you hungry?"

Fat Torrence stared at him in amazement.

"At five o'clock in the afternoon?"

"You probably won't get a chance to eat later on. Go

and get a snack now, or, if you'd rather, buy yourself some sandwiches. I want you to go to the Quai de la Mégisserie to relieve Janvier. It's the second-floor apartment. I'll send someone to relieve you first thing in the morning. You'll find the keys on the round table in the living room.

"Watch yourself, though, because the murderer must have a key to the front door. Otherwise there would have been signs of a forced entry."

"Do you think he'll come back?"

"In this extraordinary case, anything might happen."

Maigret called Doctor Forniaux.

"Have you finished the autopsy yet?"

"I was just about to dictate my report. Would you believe it, that diminutive old woman could well have lived to be a hundred? You wouldn't find many young girls with organs in a healthier condition.

"As I suspected from the first, she was suffocated: almost certainly with a scarf with scarlet threads in it. I found one lodged in a tooth. She tried to bite through it. She almost certainly put up a struggle before she blacked out for lack of air."

"Thanks, Doctor. Let me have your report as soon as you can."

"You'll get it tomorrow, in the first mail."

Léontine Antoine did not drink; at least she kept no wines or spirits in her apartment. She ate a lot of cheese. The Chief Superintendent, standing by the window watching the traffic flow across the Pont Saint-Michel, pondered, trying to re-create the details of her life. A string of barges went under the bridge, drawn by a tug with an enormous white clover leaf painted on the funnel.

The sky was a delicate pink, faintly tinged with blue;

the trees, not yet in full leaf, were pale green and full of twittering birds.

It was at this moment that the policeman who had first noticed the old lady arrived, asking to speak to the Chief Superintendent.

"I don't know if it's important—I've only just seen the photograph in the papers—but, you see, I recognized the old lady at once. What I mean to say is, I saw her almost a week ago. I was on guard duty at the main gate. She wandered up and down outside for some time, gazing up at the windows and peering into the forecourt. I thought she was about to speak to me, but then she seemed to change her mind, and she went away without saying a word.

"She was back the next day, and this time she plucked up the courage to ask me where your office was. I told her, and, before I knew it, she was gone. I didn't attempt to stop her. I thought she was just an ordinary tourist. We get so many of them. . . .

"The following day I was off duty. Lecoeur was on in my place, and he saw her go through the gate and make straight for the Police Headquarters entrance. She looked so determined that he didn't even think to ask her if she had an appointment."

"Thanks. Let me have a statement in writing, and one from Lecoeur, too."

So several days had gone by before she had been able to pluck up the courage to ask to see Chief Superintendent Maigret. And he had palmed her off on Lapointe, whom she had at first taken to be his son.

But this had not prevented her from stopping the Chief Superintendent later, in the street.

Old Joseph was knocking at the door. There was no mistaking that distinctive knock. He opened it before Maigret had time to say, "Come in."

He handed him a slip bearing the name "Billy Louette."

Yet, only a few hours earlier, the masseuse had claimed that her son was away, somewhere on the Riviera.

"Bring him in, Joseph."

Chapter 3

"You've been trying to get in touch with me, I suppose?"

"Not yet. I understood from your mother that you were on the Riviera."

"Oh! Pay no attention to her. . . . May I smoke?"

"Certainly, if you wish."

The young man appeared by no means overawed. The precincts of Police Headquarters held no terrors for him, and, as far as he was concerned, Maigret was a policeman, like any other.

But the impression he created was not that of a rebel or exhibitionist. His red hair was on the long side, but still neat. He wore a check shirt, suède coat, beige corduroy trousers, and moccasins.

"As soon as I read about my aunt in the paper, I felt sure you would want to see me."

"I'm very glad you've come."

He bore no resemblance to the masseuse. While she was tall and heavily built, with shoulders like a man, he was

57

small-boned and rather thin, with eyes as blue as peri-
winkles. Maigret, seated at his desk, motioned to the
armchair facing him.

"Thank you. What exactly happened yesterday? There's
very little in the papers."

"We know no more than they have reported, which
is that she was murdered."

"Was anything stolen?"

"Apparently not."

"Anyway, she never kept much money in the apartment."

"How do you know that?"

"I used to go to see her occasionally."

"When funds were low?"

"That goes without saying. There was nothing else for
us to talk about. We had no interests in common."

"Did she give you money?"

"As a rule, a hundred-franc note, but it wouldn't have
done to ask too often."

"You're a musician, I believe."

"Of sorts, yes. I play the guitar. I work with a small
group. We call ourselves the Beastly Buggers."

"Do you make a living out of it?"

"We have our ups and downs. Sometimes we get a booking at a high-class night club; at other times we play in
cafés. What did my mother say about me?"

"Nothing in particular."

"Don't imagine she's overflowing with motherly love.
For one thing, we're so very different. She thinks of nothing but money; saving up for her old age, she calls it. If
she could do without food, she would, to have more in the
bank."

"Was she fond of your aunt?"

"She couldn't stand her. I've heard her say quite often, 'I do believe the old fool will live forever!' "

"Why should she have wished her dead?"

"For the money, of course. The old woman, with her two widow's pensions, must have had a tidy sum put away.

"Mind you, I was fond of the old girl. And I think she liked me. She always insisted on making coffee and serving it to me with biscuits.

" 'I'm sure there are days when you can't afford to eat. Why don't you take a training course of some sort and get a decent job?' she'd say.

"My mother felt the same way. She'd made up her mind before I was fifteen what she wanted me to be. . . . She had dreams of turning me into an orthopedist.

" 'They're in such demand that patients often have to wait a month for an appointment. It's not uninteresting, and the pay is good.' "

"When did you last go to see your great-aunt?"

"About three weeks ago. We'd been to London to look around. We were hoping to get a booking, but they've got all the groups they want over there, and most of them are a lot better than we are. So we had to give up and come home, and I went to see the old girl."

"Did she give you your hundred francs?"

"Yes. And my biscuits."

"Where do you live?"

"I move around a good deal. Sometimes I'm with a girl, sometimes on my own, as I am at the moment. I've got a furnished room in a small hotel on the Rue Mouffetard."

"Are you working?"

"In a manner of speaking. Do you know the Bongo?"

Maigret shook his head. The young man seemed surprised that there should be anyone who had not heard of the Bongo.

"It's a little café-restaurant on Place Maubert. The proprietor comes from Auvergne. It didn't take him long to see what was happening in the Saint-Germain district. He got the idea to set up a hippie joint, and, to attract them, he sometimes lets them have free drinks. He's always glad to give a free dinner, and a few francs extra, to any performer willing to put on a show. That's us. We do two or three shows a night. And then there's Line. She's a singer. She's got a fabulous voice.

"That's how he gets the customers. They come in droves to get a closer look at the notorious hippies, and when we tell them we don't smoke pot or hash, they don't believe us."

"Do you intend to go on playing?"

"Sure. It's the only thing I care about. I've even started composing, though I haven't found my style yet. I can say this, at any rate, I didn't kill the old girl. First of all, killing people isn't my thing, and secondly, I'd have known I'd be a prime suspect."

"Did you have a key to the apartment?"

"What for?"

"Where were you round about six yesterday evening?"

"In bed."

"Alone?"

"Alone at last, yes. We'd been at the Bongo nearly all night. I picked up a swinging chick. She was Scandinavian —Danish or Swedish, I think. We'd had a lot to drink. Early in the morning I took her back to my room. And it wasn't until three o'clock in the afternoon that I was able to get some sleep.

"Sometime later I felt the bed creak and heard noises. I was still half asleep. All I knew was that there was no longer anyone beside me in the bed.

"I felt battered, drained, I had the most terrific hangover. I didn't get up until after nine."

"In other words, no one saw you between, say, five and eight?"

"That's right."

"Could you get in touch with the girl again?"

"If she's not at the Bongo tonight, she'll be in some other joint nearby."

"Was she someone you already knew?"

"No."

"She's a new one, then?"

"It's not like that at all. They drift in, and they drift out. I told you we'd been to London. Well, we went to Copenhagen, too. Wherever we go we make friends right away."

"Do you know her name?"

"Only her Christian name. It's Hilda. I also happen to know that her father is some bigshot in the Civil Service."

"How old is she?"

"Twenty-two, or so she said. I don't know who it was she had arranged to meet. If she hadn't, she'd probably have stayed with me for weeks. That's how it goes. Then, after a time, you drift apart, without quite knowing why. No hard feelings, though."

"Tell me about you and your mother."

"As I said, we don't get along."

"She brought you up, didn't she?"

"Not from choice. That was one of the things she had against the old girl. She hoped she'd offer to look after me. Since she had to go out to work, she dumped me in a day nursery every morning and picked me up on her way home at night. It was the same when I was at school.

"She didn't want a kid in the way, especially when there was a man around. I was an embarrassment."

"Were there many men?"

"They came and went. One lived with us for six months. He spent most of the day loafing around the house. I was made to call him 'Daddy'."

"Didn't he have a job?"

"He was supposed to be a traveling salesman, but he did damn little traveling. At other times, I'd hear noises in the night, but there was no one there in the morning. They were nearly all young men, especially recently.

"About two weeks ago, I ran into her on the Boulevard Saint-Germain. She was with a guy I've often seen around the night clubs. Everyone calls him Le Grand Marcel."

"Do you know him?"

"Not personally, but he's rumored to be a pimp. And then, of course, she's fond of the bottle."

He was cynical, yet, at the same time, refreshingly candid.

"Look, I'm not saying I suspect my mother of having killed the old girl. She is what she is, and I am what I am, and there's no changing either of us. Maybe I'll become a star, and maybe I'll be a flop, like so many others in the Saint-Germain quarter. Was there anything else you wanted to ask me?"

"A number of things, I'm sure, but for the moment they escape me. Are you happy as you are?"

"Most of the time, yes."

"Wouldn't you have been better off if you had done as

your mother wished and become an orthopedist? You would probably have been married, with children, by this time."

"It wouldn't suit me. Maybe later."

"How did you feel when you heard of your great-aunt's death?"

"It shook me. I didn't know her well. To me she was just a very old woman, who should have been put underground long ago. But still I was fond of her. I liked her eyes and her smile.

" 'Eat up,' she used to say.

"And she used to watch me eat those biscuits of hers with a kind of loving concern. Apart from my mother, I was all she had in the way of a family.

" 'Are you really quite set on wearing your hair so long?' she'd say.

"That was the thing that upset her most.

" 'It makes you look different from what you really are. Because underneath it all, you're a good boy.'

"When is the funeral?"

"I can't say yet. Leave your address with me, and I'll let you know. It will probably be the day after tomorrow. It really depends on the Examining Magistrate."

"Did she suffer, do you think?"

"She put up very little resistance. Do you, by any chance, own a red scarf, or at least one with red in it?"

"I never wear a scarf. Why?"

"No reason. I'm feeling my way, that's all."

"Do you suspect anyone?"

"I wouldn't go so far as that."

"Could it be some sort of perverted sex crime?"

"Why pick on Madame Antoine in particular, and why

attack her at home, with the building swarming with people? No, the murderer was looking for something."

"Money?"

"I'm not sure. If he was someone who knew her, he would have known that she never had more than a few francs in cash. Besides, he visited the apartment several times while the old lady was out. Do you happen to know if she owned anything of value?"

"She had a few pieces of jewelry, nothing worth much, just trinkets given her by her two husbands."

Maigret had seen them: a garnet ring, with earrings to match, a gold bracelet, and a small gold watch.

There were, in the same box, a pearl tiepin and a pair of silver cuff links, which must have belonged to Caramé. All old-fashioned stuff and with virtually no resale value.

"Did she have any papers?"

"What do you mean by papers? She was just an ordinary old woman, who lived a quiet life with her first husband and then, later, with her second. Caramé died before I was born, so I never met him, but I knew the other one, Joseph Antoine. He was a nice man...."

Maigret stood up with a sigh.

"Do you visit your mother often?"

"Hardly ever."

"You don't happen to know, do you, whether she's living alone at the moment, or whether this Monsieur Marcel you mentioned is with her?"

"I don't, I'm afraid."

"I'm very grateful to you for having come, Monsieur Louette. I'd like to see your show some night, if I can find the time."

"About eleven is the best time to come."

"I'm usually in bed by then."

"Am I still a suspect?"

"Until I have evidence to the contrary, everyone is suspect, but you are no more suspect than anyone else."

Maigret shut the door behind the young man and went across to lean out the window. It was already dusk. Everything looked a little blurred. He had learned a great many new facts, but none of them was of any use to him.

What could anybody possibly want from the old woman's home on the Quai de la Mégisserie?

She had lived in the same apartment for over forty years. There was no mystery about her first husband, and after he died, she had lived on there alone for nearly ten years.

As far as one could tell, there had been no mystery about her second husband, either. He had been dead for years, and since his death, she had led an uneventful life, seeing no one except her niece and great-nephew.

Why had no one ever tried to break into her apartment before? Was it because what the intruder was looking for had been there only a short time?

With a little grunt and a shrug, he opened the door to the inspectors' duty room.

"See you all tomorrow."

Traveling home on the bus, he reflected that there was no other profession quite like his own. He did not know the names of his fellow passengers, yet he never knew from one moment to the next if he might have to shoulder his way into the life of any of them.

He rather liked the young man with the long red hair, but his only interest in the mother was to find out the answers to several very personal questions.

As usual, Madame Maigret had the door open almost before he was across the landing.

"You look worried."

"And with good reason. I'm caught up in something I simply don't understand."

"The murder of the old woman?"

Naturally she had read the paper and heard the news broadcast.

"Did you ever see her alive?"

"Yes."

"What was she like?"

"I thought she was mad, or at least not quite right in the head. She was a tiny little thing; she looked as if a puff of wind could blow her away. She begged me to help her. The way she talked you'd have thought I was the only person in the world who could."

"Didn't you do anything?"

"I couldn't detail an inspector to keep watch on her night and day.

"There was so little to go on. All she could say was that, once or twice, she had come home to her apartment to find some of her things very slightly out of place.

"I confess I thought she was imagining things, or that her memory was playing tricks on her. All the same, I had made up my mind to go to see her, if only to reassure her. Yesterday she must have got home earlier than usual and found the intruder still in her apartment.

"It was all too easy to silence her. He needed no more than a scarf or a dishcloth held over her face for a minute or two. . . ."

"Did she have any family?"

"Just one niece and a great-nephew. I've seen them

both. The niece is a big, hefty woman, more like a man. She's a masseuse. The young man, on the other hand, is small and thin and redheaded. He plays the guitar in a night club on Place Maubert."

"Has anything been stolen?"

"Impossible to say. There's just one thing, and it's not much to go on. She used to keep a revolver in her bedside-table drawer, but it's not there now."

"Surely no one would kill an old woman in cold blood just for the sake of a revolver? And it wouldn't take several visits to find it."

"Let's eat!"

They dined facing one another across the table near the open window. Neither of them felt like looking at television. It was a very mild evening. The air was still. As the night drew on, a pleasant, light breeze blew up, creating a faint whisper among the leaves of the trees.

"Since you weren't home for lunch, I've warmed up the lamb stew."

"I'm delighted to hear it."

He ate with relish, but his thoughts were elsewhere. He could not forget his meeting with the old lady in gray, on the sidewalk of the Quai des Orfèvres. He could still see her looking up at him, her eyes bright with trust and admiration.

"Why don't you forget it, just for tonight?"

"I wish I could. I can't help myself. If there's one thing I hate, it's letting people down, and, as things turned out, it cost the poor old dear her life."

"Let's go for a walk."

He agreed. There was no point in moping around the apartment all evening. Besides, it was his way—one might almost call it an obsession—when he was on a case, to establish a routine and adhere to it day after day.

They walked to the Bastille, and sat for a little while on a café terrace. A long-haired youth with a guitar strummed as he made his way among the tables, followed by a black-eyed girl holding out a saucer.

Needless to say, he was reminded of the redhead who, no doubt, when times were hard, had also done his stint as a café entertainer.

Maigret's contribution was more than generous, a fact that did not escape his wife. She said nothing, however, but merely smiled to herself. They sat on for some time, in silence, gazing out at the lights of the city.

He puffed gently at his pipe. At one point, he almost suggested going to the Bongo. But what was the use? What could he hope to find out beyond what he already knew?

The tenants of the building on the Quai de la Mégisserie were also suspects. Any of them might have known the old lady better than they were prepared to admit. It would have been easy enough for anyone to take a wax impression of the lock and get a key cut to fit it.

But why? This was the question that haunted Maigret. Why? Why? What was the object of those repeated visits to the apartment? Certainly not for the sake of the few francs the old lady kept there. There had been several hundred francs in the chest of drawers, just lying there for anyone to take. But they had not been taken. Maigret had found them inside the cover of the old lady's Post Office Savings book.

"Tomorrow I'll start inquiring into the lives and backgrounds of the two husbands."

It was absurd, really, especially taking into account how long the second husband had been dead.

Nevertheless, there was a secret somewhere, a secret important enough to warrant the taking of a human life.

"Shall we go?"

He had drunk a small glass of Calvados and had just stopped himself in time from ordering another. His friend Pardon would have been displeased with him for even contemplating it. Maigret remembered his solemn warning just in time:

"One can drink wines and spirits for years without any ill effects, but a time comes when the system will no longer tolerate them."

He shrugged, got up, and threaded his way between the tables. In the street, Madame Maigret took his arm. Boulevard Beaumarchais. Rue Servan. At last Boulevard Richard-Lenoir and their much-loved, shabby old apartment.

Contrary to his expectations, he fell asleep almost at once.

The night passed without incident in the apartment on the Quai de la Mégisserie, and corpulent Torrence was able to enjoy a full night's sleep in the old lady's armchair.

At eight in the morning, Loutrie arrived to relieve him and found the concierge deep in conversation with a newspaper reporter.

At nine, Maigret, brooding and grumpy, pushed open the door of the inspectors' room and beckoned to Janvier and Lapointe.

"On second thought, Lucas, you'd better come, too."

He sat down at his desk and proceeded to make a ceremony of choosing a pipe from his pipe rack.

"Well, men, we're no further than we were this time yesterday. Since we don't seem to be able to find any lead in the present, we're going to do a little probing into the past. I want you to go to the Hôtel de Ville department store, Lucas, the hardware department. There must still be people working there who knew old Antoine.

"Ask as many questions as you like. Find out all you can about the old boy, his personality, his interests, everything."

"Will do, Chief. Wouldn't it be better if I got the consent of the management first? They couldn't very well refuse, and the members of the staff would probably feel freer to talk than if I approached them in an underhand way."

"Agreed. As for you, Janvier, I want you to go to City Hall and do the same for Caramé. It will be more difficult, because he's been dead so much longer. If any of his contemporaries are still living in retirement, get their addresses and go to see them."

All this was just routine, of course, but sometimes routine paid off.

"Lapointe, I want you with me."

Downstairs in the forecourt, the young inspector asked: "Do we need a car?"

"No, we're just going across the bridge to the Rue Saint-André-des-Arts. A car would only slow us up."

It was an old building, similar to that on the Quai de la Mégisserie and, indeed, to all the other buildings in the neighborhood. There was a picture framer's shop to the right of it, and a candy shop to the left. The glass door of the lodge was accessible from the entrance hall, which ran right through to a courtyard at the back.

Maigret went into the lodge and introduced himself to the concierge. She was a plump little woman, with a high color. As a child, she must have had dimples. Indeed, she still did when she smiled.

"I thought someone would be coming from the police."

"Why?"

"When I read what happened to that poor old lady, I had an idea that the niece they spoke of was one of my tenants."

"Angèle Louette, you mean?"

"Yes."

"Has she ever mentioned her aunt?"

"She's not very communicative, but, even so, she does drop in for a chat occasionally. I remember once we were discussing people who don't pay their bills. She remarked that sometimes it was the high-ups who were the worst. Some of her own clients were in that class, she said, and she dared not press them too hard; they had too much influence.

" 'It's a mercy that I've got my aunt's money to look forward to!'

"She brought it out just like that. She told me that the old lady had been widowed twice, and that she was drawing two pensions and must have quite a bit put away."

"Does she have many visitors?"

The concierge looked uncomfortable.

"What do you mean?"

"Does she often entertain women friends?"

"Not women friends, no."

"Clients?"

"They don't come to her; she goes to them."

"What about men?"

"Well, I don't suppose there's any harm in telling you. There are men from time to time. There was even one who stayed for nearly six months. He was ten years younger than she was, and he did all the housework and the shopping."

"Is she in now?"

"She went out about an hour ago. She always starts on her rounds pretty early. But there is someone up there."

"One of her regular visitors?"

"I don't know. She got in rather late last night. After I'd let her in, I heard two sets of footsteps. And if the person who was with her had left the building, I'd have known."

"Does it happen often?"

"Not often. Just once in a while."

"What about her son?"

"He hardly ever comes here. I haven't seen him in months. He looks like a hippie, but he's a good boy, really."

"Thank you. We'd better have a look around up there, I think."

There was no elevator. The apartment was at the back, overlooking the courtyard. The door was not locked; Maigret and Lapointe went in, finding themselves in a living room fitted out with fairly new, mass-produced furniture.

There wasn't a sound to be heard. There was a door, obviously leading to the bedroom. Maigret opened it and saw a man asleep in the double bed. He opened his eyes and stared in amazement at the Chief Superintendent.

"What is it? What do you want?"

"It's really Angèle Louette I came to see, but since you're here ..."

"Aren't you ..."

"That's right, Chief Superintendent Maigret. We've met before, years ago. In those days you worked in a bar on the Rue Fontaine. You were known as Le Grand Marcel, if I'm not mistaken."

"I still am. Would you kindly leave me for a moment so that I can get dressed? I don't have anything on."

"Don't trouble yourself on my account."

He was tall, thin, and bony. Hastily he slipped on a pair of trousers and searched for his slippers, which he eventually found under the bed.

"You know, it isn't the way you think, between me and Angèle. We're just good friends. Yesterday we spent the evening together, and, by the end of it, I wasn't feeling too good. So, instead of trekking right across Paris to my own place on Boulevard des Batignolles ..."

Maigret opened the wardrobe. There were two men's suits in the hanging section and, in the drawers, several shirts and two or three pairs of socks and underpants.

"Can I make myself a cup of coffee?"

Maigret followed Le Grand Marcel into the kitchen and watched him make the coffee. It was obvious that he knew his way around.

"There's nothing to tell. I've had my ups and downs, as you very well know. I'm not a pimp, and never have been, in spite of what people say. You know yourself that the charges were dropped for lack of evidence."

"How old are you?"

"Thirty-five."

"How old is she?"

"I don't know exactly. Fiftyish, I suppose. Yes, she could be fifty."

"The great love of your life, no doubt!"

"We understand one another. She can't do without me. I've kept away from her for as long as a week before now, and when that happens, she comes looking for me in all my old hangouts."

"Where were you in the late afternoon of the day before yesterday?"

"The day before yesterday? Let me think. I must have been somewhere in the neighborhood, because I was due to meet Angèle at seven."

"She didn't mention it."

"It probably slipped her mind. We had a dinner date. I had an apéritif on the terrace of a café on Boulevard Saint-Germain."

"And did she meet you at seven, as arranged?"

"She may have been a bit late. Yes, come to think of it, she was very late. She was kept waiting by one of her clients. It must have been about half past seven when she arrived."

"Did you have dinner together, as arranged?"

"Yes, and afterward we went to a movie. You can check on it if you don't believe me. The restaurant is Lucio's on the Quai de la Tournelle. They know me well there."

"Where are you working now?"

"To tell you the truth, I'm between jobs. It's not easy to find work these days."

"Does she keep you?"

"That's a nasty remark. You've no reason to go out of your way to offend me. For years you people have been trying to pin something on me, and I'm not guilty, I tell you. It's true she lends me a little money now and then. It's the most she can do. She doesn't earn all that much herself."

"Were you intending to sleep all morning?"

"I'm expecting her back any minute. She's got an hour free between two appointments. She went to see you yesterday and told you all she knew.

"What I want to know is what you're doing here now."

"Taking advantage of the opportunity to make your acquaintance!"

"Would you mind waiting in the other room while I take a shower?"

"You have my permission to shave, too," retorted Maigret, a little unkindly.

Lapointe could not get over the presence of such a man in Angèle Louette's apartment.

"He's been arrested four or five times for procuring. He was also suspected of being tied up with that Corsican gang that caused so much commotion in Paris a few years back. But he's as slippery as an eel, and nothing was ever proved."

Someone was coming up the stairs. The door opened. Madame Antoine's niece stood transfixed in the doorway.

"Do come in! I was hoping for a word with you."

She shot a furtive glance toward the bedroom door.

"Yes, he's in there. He's just having a shower and a shave."

Defeated, she shut the door with a resigned shrug.

"After all, it's nobody's business but my own. Well, is it?"

"You may be right."

"What do you mean?"

"He just happens to be an old acquaintance of mine, and in the past he's had one or two brushes with the law."

"Are you telling me he's a thief?"

"No. At least, not to my knowledge. But, in the days when he was a barman, there were always two or three women working for him, not to mention the lady in charge of the establishment."

"I don't believe you. If what you say is true, he'd have been sent to prison."

"The only reason he wasn't is that we didn't have enough evidence."

"You still haven't told me why you're here."

"First, let me ask you a question. Yesterday, when you mentioned your son to me, you told me he was on the Riviera. . . ."

"I said I thought he was."

"In fact he's still in Paris, and he's been good enough to tell me some very interesting things."

"I'm well aware that he dislikes me."

"The same way you disliked your aunt?"

"I can't imagine what he's been saying. He's full of crazy notions. Mark my words, he'll come to no good."

"On the day your aunt died you had an appointment with Le Grand Marcel for seven o'clock on the terrace of a café on Boulevard Saint-Germain."

"If that's what he says, it's the truth."

"What time did you actually get there?"

She was caught off her guard for a moment. She hesitated, then said:

"I was kept waiting by one of my clients. I must have arrived at about half past seven."

"Where did you have dinner?"

"At an Italian restaurant on the Quai de la Tournelle, Chez Lucio."

"And then?"

"We went to a movie at the Saint-Michel."

"Do you know what time your aunt was murdered?"

"No. I know nothing but what you told me."

"It was between five and half past seven."

"What's that supposed to mean?"

"Do you own a revolver?"

"Certainly not. I wouldn't know what to do with it."

Le Grand Marcel emerged from the bedroom, nonchalantly tying a knot in his blue silk tie. He was freshly shaved and wearing a white shirt.

"What do you know?" he said, making a joke of it. "I woke up suddenly to find these gentlemen standing at the foot of the bed, towering over me. For a moment, I thought I was in a gangster film."

"Do you own a revolver?" barked Maigret.

"No, sir! Can you think of a surer way of getting jailed?"

"You live on Boulevard des Batignolles, I believe. What number?"

"Twenty-seven."

"I'm much obliged to you both for your co-operation. As for your aunt, mademoiselle, the Forensic Laboratory has completed its work, so you are at liberty to send for the body and make arrangements for the funeral at any time that suits you."

"Do I have to pay for it out of my own pocket?"

"That's entirely up to you. As her next of kin you will inherit more than enough to give her a decent burial."

"What should I do? Should I see a lawyer?"

"If I were you, I'd see her bank manager. He'll tell you all you need to know. If you don't know the name of her bank, you'll find it on her bankbook in the chest of drawers in the living room."

"Thank you."

"Don't mention it.

"And don't forget to let me know the date and time of the funeral."

She was looking at him unblinkingly. He had seldom seen eyes colder or more steely than hers. As for Marcel, he was doing his best to look as though all this were no concern of his.

"See you later, Monsieur Maigret," he said with studied insolence.

Maigret and Lapointe left. The Chief Superintendent stopped at the bar on the corner.

"Those two have given me a thirst," he said, and led the way in.

"A beer, please. What will you have?"

"The same."

"Two beers."

Maigret got out his handkerchief and mopped his brow.

"What a way to investigate the killing of an old lady with gray eyes! Dropping in on people and asking them a lot of more or less pointless questions! Oh, well, those two have got the laugh on us for the time being, but not for long, I hope!"

Lapointe wisely said nothing, but it troubled him to see the Chief so moody.

"Mind you, it's always like this at some stage. You're stuck, and you don't know what to do next. Until something happens—often it's something quite trivial, and you don't realize its significance at the time. . . ."

"Cheers!"

"Cheers!"

It was still quite early. Maigret was heartened by the sight of so many busy housewives bustling from shop to shop. They were not far from the Buci market, of which he was particularly fond.

"Come on."

"Where are we going?"

"Back to the office. We'll see whether Lucas and Janvier have had better luck."

Janvier was back, but not Lucas.

"No trouble at all, Chief. His successor is still there. He knew Caramé extremely well, right from the time when he joined the service."

"Go on."

"It's all perfectly open and above board, except that they all called Caramé 'His Majesty' behind his back. He had an air about him, and he was very fastidious in his dress. He was highly conscious of the dignity of his position. He had been promised the Legion of Honor and was greatly looking forward to receiving it. He never missed an opportunity to appear in a morning coat, in which he looked particularly well.

"His brother was a Colonel. He was killed in Indo-China. Caramé was always ready to talk about 'My brother, the Colonel.' "

"Is that all?"

"More or less. Apparently, he had no vices. His one great sorrow was that he had no children. One of the messengers, a very old man, told me something, though he couldn't guarantee that it was true. . . .

"After they'd been married three or four years, he sent his wife to a gynecologist, who subsequently asked to see him, the inference being that it was he, not she, who was sterile. From that time onward, he never referred to the subject of children again."

Maigret paced up and down his office, still wearing the same surly expression. From time to time, he would pause by the window and gaze at the Seine, as though calling the river to witness that, of all men, he was the most put upon.

There was a knock at the door. It was Lucas. He was out of breath, having taken the stairs at a run.

"Take your time."

"I found a man in the hardware department who had been Antoine's number two. He's sixty now, and head of the department."

"What did he say?"

"It looks as if Antoine was a bit of a nut. In the nicest way, of course. It seems he had a bee in his bonnet. When anyone asked him what he did for a living, he invariably replied that he was an inventor.

"And it's a fact that he patented a very ingenious design for a can opener and sold it to a hardware manufacturer. He invented several other things, too. . . ."

"Such as a potato peeler?"

"How did you know?"

"I saw one in the apartment on the Quai de la Mégisserie."

"He was always at work on some new invention or other. He had set up a workshop in the apartment and spent every spare minute puttering around in it."

"I've seen the workshop, too. Were all his inventions household gadgets? Didn't he ever try his hand at anything more ambitious?"

"Not as far as the man I spoke to knew. But he seems to have had a way of wagging his head and dropping dark hints, such as:

" 'One day I'll come up with something really big, something that will make me famous.' "

"Did he go into any detail?"

"No. Except, when he was on his hobbyhorse, he was rather reserved, although he was very conscientious in his work. He didn't drink. He never went out at night. He seemed very fond of his wife, fond of her rather than in love with her, which isn't surprising, considering that they were both well on in years. They got along well and had great respect for one another. The man I spoke to had been to dinner twice at the apartment, and he was impressed by the pleasant, homey atmosphere.

" 'She was a charming woman,' he said. 'Such distinction! There was just one thing I found a little embarrassing. When she talked of her husband, one couldn't be quite sure whether she meant her first or her second. I had the feeling that the two had become confused in her mind.' "

"Anything else?"

"No, Chief, that's all."

"There's only one thing we can be sure of. Until quite

recently a revolver was kept in the old lady's bedside-table drawer. And it isn't there now. It's vanished.

"I feel like paying a call at Boulevard des Batignolles. Care to come with me, Lapointe? Whichever car you pick, make sure it isn't the one with the engine rattle."

Before leaving his office, he put his pipe in the rack and selected another.

Chapter 4

The fake marble plaque beside the entrance to the little hotel bore the legend:

FURNISHED ROOMS FOR RENT
BY THE DAY, THE WEEK, OR THE MONTH.
ALL MOD. CONS.

Most of the rooms were rented to monthly tenants, and the "mod. cons." consisted of a wash basin in every room and a bathroom shared by two floors.

Inside, on the right, was a desk, and behind it a row of pigeonholes and a board with a great many keys hanging from hooks.

"Is Le Grand Marcel in his room?"

"Monsieur Marcel? He's just gone up. That's his car at the door."

It was a bright-red convertible, several years old. Two teen-age boys were inspecting it, if not with envy, at least with interest. No doubt they were wondering how fast it could go.

"Has he lived here long?"

"Over a year. He's a very pleasant gentleman."

"I take it he seldom sleeps in his room."

"He usually gets home early in the morning, which isn't surprising, seeing that he's a barman in a night club."

"Does he ever bring a girl?"

"Not often. And, anyway, it's none of my business."

The landlord was fat, with two or three bristly chins. He was wearing a pair of very old, misshapen bedroom slippers.

"What floor?"

"Second. Room number twenty-three. I hope you're not going to cause trouble. I know who you are. I don't much like having policemen tramping around the place."

"You don't have anything to hide, do you?"

"With your bunch, one can never tell."

Maigret went upstairs, followed by Lapointe. Dangling from the banister was a cardboard notice, which read:

PLEASE WIPE YOUR FEET

And underneath, written in by hand:

NO COOKING IS PERMITTED IN THE BEDROOMS

Maigret knew what that meant. No doubt every single tenant had smuggled in his own alcohol stove, on which to heat up the ready-cooked food that he regularly bought from the nearest delicatessen.

He knocked at the door of number twenty-three. There was a sound of approaching footsteps, and the door was flung open with some violence.

"Jesus!" exclaimed Le Grand Marcel. "You here already!"

"Were you expecting us?"

"Once the police start butting in, they're sure to turn up any old time."

"Are you leaving here?"

There was a suitcase on the floor, and another on the bed, into which the ex-barman had been stuffing his clothes when they arrived.

"Yes. I'm quitting. I've had just about enough."

"Enough of what?"

"Of that female Sergeant-Major."

"Have you quarreled with her?"

"You could say that. She called me every filthy name she could think of, and all because I was still in bed when you arrived. She may be a masseuse who's got to be up bright and early to go poking and kneading people in their beds, but I'm not."

"That doesn't explain why you're giving up your lodgings."

"I'm not just giving up my lodgings, I'm giving up altogether. I'm off to Toulon. I've got friends there, real friends. They'll fix me up with something right away."

Maigret recognized, folded on top of one of the cases, one of the suits he had seen earlier in the day, hanging in the wardrobe in the apartment on the Rue Saint-André-des-Arts. Le Grand Marcel was wearing the other. His surname was Montrond, but no one ever called him by it. Even his landlord addressed him as Monsieur Marcel.

"Is that red car parked outside yours?"

"She isn't worth much, she's almost ten years old, but she still keeps going."

"I take it you intend to drive to Toulon?"

"That's correct. Unless you take it into your heads to stop me."

"Why should we want to do that?"

"You tell me. You're the cop."

"Just one thing: have you ever been to the apartment on Rue de la Mégisserie?"

"What for? To pay my respects to the old girl?

" 'Greetings, dear lady. I'm your niece's boyfriend. Since I'm down on my luck at the moment, she's keeping me. She can't live without a man in bed. She's a whore all right. and it was a great mistake to get mixed up with her.' "

He went on calmly packing his suitcases, looking through all the drawers to make sure he had not forgotten anything. He took out a camera, and he also had a record player.

"Where can we get in touch with you in Toulon?"

"Write to me in care of Bob, Bar de l'Amiral, Quai de Stalingrad. He's the barman, and a very old friend of mine. Do you think you'll be needing me again?"

"You never know."

He had not yet closed the suitcases. Maigret felt around in them but found nothing of interest.

"How much did you get out of her?"

"The Sergeant-Major? Five hundred francs. And that, mark you, was only on condition that I wouldn't stay away too long. You never can tell with her. One minute she's cursing you up and down, telling you to beat it, and the next she's whimpering that she can't live without you."

"*Bon voyage!*" Maigret said with a sigh, as he made for the door.

On his way out, he paused at the desk and said to the landlord:

"It looks as if you're about to lose one of your tenants."

"So he tells me. He's going to spend a few weeks in the South."

"Is he keeping his room?"

"No, but I'll surely be able to fit him in somewhere."

The two men drove back to the Quai des Orfèvres, and Maigret lost no time in putting a call through to Toulon.

"Would you get me Superintendent Marella? Maigret, Police Headquarters, Paris, speaking."

It was pleasant to hear the familiar voice of his old colleague. They had joined the Force at about the same time, and now Marella was the senior man in Toulon.

"How are things with you?"

"Can't complain."

"Do you know the Bar de l'Amiral?"

"Don't I! It's the favorite hangout of all the crooks."

"And a man by the name of Bob?"

"The barman. They all use him as an accommodation address."

"Sometime tonight or tomorrow, a fellow called Marcel Montrond will show up in Toulon. I have an idea he'll make straight for l'Amiral. I'd be much obliged if you'd put a tail on him."

"What's your interest in him?"

"It may be nothing. It may be something very serious indeed. I don't know. All I know is, he's mixed up in some way in a case that's giving me a monumental headache."

"The old lady at the Quai de la Mégisserie?"

"Yes."

"A funny business. I know only what I've heard on the radio and read in the papers. Even so, it strikes me as mighty odd. Have you caught up with the kid who plays the guitar?"

"Yes, but I don't think he's our man. At the moment, I don't have a shred of evidence on any of them, and I can't for the life of me see any reason at all why the poor old woman should have been killed. . . ."

"I'll be in touch. This Marcel fellow wouldn't by any chance be a character known as Le Grand Marcel?"

"That's the one."

"He's a bit of a gigolo on the side, isn't he? He's quite well known around these parts, and he always seems to latch on to some woman or other."

"Many thanks. I look forward to hearing from you."

As soon as he had put down the receiver, the telephone rang.

"Chief Superintendent Maigret?"

"Yes."

"Angèle Louette speaking. First of all, I thought you'd like to know that I've given that dead beat his marching orders."

"I know. He's on his way to Toulon."

From her momentary silence, he could tell it was a shock to her.

"Please believe me, he's not my type at all. I won't be taken in so easily next time."

"What do you have against him?"

"He sponges off women and loafs around in bed most of the day—and not even in his own bed! I had a job getting rid of him. He'd still be here if I hadn't paid him off."

"I know."

"He surely wouldn't boast about it?"

"He certainly did, and, incidentally, he called you the 'Sergeant-Major.'"

"The other thing was about the funeral. It'll be tomorrow morning. The body will be back at the Quai de la Mégisserie sometime this afternoon. Since my aunt had no friends, I won't be turning the place into a memorial chapel. The funeral will be tomorrow at ten."

"Is there going to be a church service?"

"Just a memorial prayer at Notre-Dame-des-Blancs-Manteaux. Have you got any further with your inquiries?"

"No."

"Do you have my son's address?"

"He did leave it with me, yes."

"I'd like to let him know. He may want to attend his great-aunt's funeral."

"He's staying at the Hôtel des Îles et du Bon Pasteur, Rue Mouffetard."

"I'm much obliged to you."

Maigret, familiar with the ways of Examining Magistrates, knew that they did not like to be kept waiting, so, as soon as he could, he let himself through the door between Police Headquarters and the Law Courts. The corridors of the Offices of the Examining Magistrates were lined with benches, on which sat witnesses waiting their turn and, here and there, handcuffed prisoners between two wardens.

Judge Libart was alone in his room except for his clerk.

"Any news, Chief Superintendent? How are we getting on with your very special case?" He rubbed his hands together, obviously in good humor. "As you know, it's my policy to leave you in peace to get on with the job. All the same, I trust you have made some progress?"

"None at all."

"No likely suspects?"

"Not really, and nothing much to go on, except that the intruder was searching for something when the old lady came back unexpectedly and found him."

"Money?"

"I don't think so."

"Jewelry?"

"She had nothing worth stealing."

"A lunatic?"

"Not very likely. Whoever it was had searched the apartment several times before the afternoon of the crime. That doesn't look to me like the behavior of a lunatic."

"A family affair, perhaps? Someone in too much of a hurry to get whatever the old lady had to leave?"

"That's a possibility, but a somewhat remote one. The old lady's sole heir is her niece. She's a masseuse, and quite comfortably off."

"Don't let it get you down."

Maigret forced a smile.

"I'm sorry. It's just that I seem to have come to a dead end. The funeral is tomorrow."

"Will you be going?"

"Yes. I always make a point of it. I've been put on the right track before now by watching the mourners at a funeral."

He went home for lunch, and Madame Maigret, noting his preoccupied expression, was careful to ask no questions.

She went about on tiptoe and watched him anxiously as he ate the veal steak with sorrel, which she had cooked for him, knowing it to be one of his favorite dishes.

Soon after he got back to the Quai des Orfèvres, there was a knock at his door.

"Come in."

It was Lapointe.

"Sorry to bother you, Chief, but you haven't given me any instructions."

"I haven't any to give you. Do what you think best. If anything occurs to you . . ."

"I'd like another word with the man in the bird shop. Not many people would be able to enter or leave the building without being seen by him. Maybe, if I prod his memory a bit, he'll come up with something useful."

"It's up to you."

He hated himself for feeling as he did, bereft of inspiration and a prey to inertia. Thoughts buzzed in his head until he was sick of them, but none of them seemed to be leading anywhere.

Foremost in his mind was the thought that Madame Antoine had been as sane as he was himself.

Why had she hesitated so long, pacing up and down the Quai des Orfèvres, before plucking up the courage to speak to the policeman at the gate? Had she known more than she was prepared to tell?

She must have realized that her complaint—namely, that she had found some of her knickknacks almost imperceptibly displaced—was bound to be received with skepticism.

Still, she had been right. The apartment had indeed been subjected to a thorough search on several occasions.

But why? What had the intruder been looking for?

As he had explained to the Examining Magistrate, certainly not money or jewelry.

But one thing was certain: whatever it was, it was important enough to warrant the murder of the old lady, when she came back unexpectedly, while the intruder was still there.

Had he or had he not, in the end, found what he was looking for?

Was he perhaps on his way out with his booty, when he heard Madame Antoine's key in the lock?

What could a very old woman, twice-widowed, living quietly and modestly by herself, possibly possess that was worth committing murder for?

While these thoughts were going through his head, Maigret was doodling absent-mindedly on a large sheet of paper. Suddenly, he realized that he had been making a rough sketch of an old lady, not unlike Madame Antoine.

By five o'clock he was beginning to feel stifled in his office. Taking with him a photograph of Le Grand Marcel, which he had got from the Vice Squad, he set off for the Quai de la Mégisserie.

It was a poor likeness—the man appeared more hard-featured than he was in real life—but it was still recognizable. He went first to the concierge.

"Have you ever seen this man?"

She went to get her glasses, which were on the kitchen counter.

"I wouldn't really like to say, though he does seem vaguely familiar. On the other hand, there are lots of people around who look a bit like him."

"Take a closer look. If you saw him, it was probably quite recently."

"Actually, it's the suit that rings a bell. I saw a check suit like that somewhere a week or two back, but I can't for the life of me think where."

"Here, in the lodge?"

"No, I don't think so."

"In the courtyard? On the stairs?"

"Honestly, I can't say. Your inspector was here again, asking questions, just a short while ago. You wouldn't want me to start inventing things, now, would you? You know they've brought her back?"

"Madame Antoine, you mean?"

"Yes. Her niece is up there with her. She's left the door open and lit candles on either side of the bed. One or two of the tenants plucked up the courage to go to say a little prayer. If I'd had anyone to look after things here, I'd have gone to the funeral tomorrow, but I'm all by myself. My husband is in a mental hospital. He's been there for three years."

Maigret went out onto the sidewalk, where the bird cages were standing outside the shop. Monsieur Caille's son recognized him immediately.

"Hello! One of your inspectors, the young one, has been here. He just left."

"I know. I'd be obliged if you'd look carefully at this photograph."

He did so, shook his head, held it up close, and then at arm's length.

"I can't exactly say I recognize him, but there is something. . . ."

"Is it the suit?"

"No, not especially. It's his expression. That sort of devil-may-care look."

"One of your customers, perhaps?"

"Oh, no. I'm sure it's not."

"Hadn't you better show it to your father?"

"I will, of course, but he's so terribly nearsighted."
He came back shaking his head.

"He doesn't recognize him. Though you must remember
that he spends most of his time in the shop and really cares
for nothing but his birds and his fish. In fact, he's so
devoted to them that it wouldn't take much for him to
refuse to sell them."

Maigret went back into the building and climbed the
stairs to the second floor. The woman who lived opposite
Madame Antoine came out, with a string shopping bag over
her arm.

"She's there," she whispered, pointing to the half-open
door.

"I know."

"The funeral is tomorrow. It seems her first husband
bought a plot in the Montparnasse cemetery, and she
wanted to be buried beside him."

"Who knew of her wishes?"

"Her niece, no doubt. And I know she told the concierge.
She used to say that Ivry was too far out, and that she felt
lost among all those thousands of graves."

"There's something I'd like to show you. Could we go
into your apartment for a moment?"

It was very neat and tidy, somewhat darker than the
old lady's, because the windows were almost entirely ob-
scured by the overhanging branches of a tree.

"Have you ever seen this man before?"

Once again he produced the little photograph taken by
someone in Criminal Records.

"Is it someone I know?"

"I've no idea. You tell me."

"You asked me if I'd ever seen him before. Well, I certainly have, not very long ago. He was smoking a cigarette. I knew there was something missing. That's it. The cigarette."

"Take your time. Try to think back."

"It isn't one of the tradesmen, or anyone I've seen going in and out of the yard."

She was obviously doing her best.

"I suppose it's important?"

"Yes."

"Something to do with Madame Antoine?"

"I think it likely."

"So if I identify him positively, it will mean trouble for him?"

"I'm afraid so."

"You see my difficulty. I wouldn't want to get an innocent person into trouble."

"If he's innocent, we shall soon know it."

"That's not always the case. Even the police can make mistakes. Oh, well, never mind! I was on my way out. . . ."

"What day was this?"

"I don't remember. One day last week. I was going to pick up my daughter at school."

There was a little girl doing her homework in the next room.

"That would have been a little before four?"

"Or it might have been lunch time. That's what I'm trying to remember. More likely it was four, because I had my shopping bag with me, and that's when I always buy the things I need for dinner. My husband doesn't come home for lunch, and my daughter and I just have something very light.

"I was on my way downstairs, not looking where I was going, when I bumped into someone. He was coming up the stairs, three at a time. He nearly sent me flying. That's why I remember him.

"He turned around and asked me if I was hurt. I said no, it was nothing."

"Do you happen to know where he was going, which floor?"

"No. I was in a hurry. My daughter doesn't like to be kept hanging around outside the school gates, and, with all the traffic, I wouldn't dare let her come home alone."

Maigret heaved a sigh. At last, a faint ray of hope!

A moment or two later he was in the bedroom, gazing intently at the delicately modeled features of the old woman whom he had thought to be mad.

The curtains were three-quarters drawn, and the room was almost in darkness, except for a narrow strip of shimmering sunlight. Two wax candles were burning, one on either side of the bed, making everything look strange and different.

Angèle Louette was there, sitting in an armchair, silent and motionless. At first Maigret thought she was asleep, until he looked again and saw her somber eyes fixed upon him.

He stood facing the dead woman for a minute or two, to give himself time to recover, then went into the living room. It was a relief to be back in daylight. As he had expected, she came out after him.

She looked even more hard-featured than usual.

"What have you come here for?"

"To pay my last respects to your aunt."

"If you ask me, nothing is further from your mind. And the same goes for the neighbors. Only two of them bothered to put their heads around the door. Any more news of that scoundrel Marcel?"

"He got into his car and drove off to Toulon."

"Good riddance! I had trouble enough getting rid of him. I told you I had to give him five hundred francs to get him to leave?"

"That's extortion of money by threats. You could make a charge."

"Maybe I will. At any rate, if he makes any attempt to come back . . ."

"Did you know that he was here, in this building, one day last week?"

She started violently and frowned.

"Do you know what day?"

"No."

"What time of day?"

"Around four."

"Did he tell you so himself?"

"No."

"Have you asked him about it?"

"I haven't had a chance. How did he come to have your aunt's address?"

"One day, about a month ago, when we were crossing the Pont-Neuf, I pointed to the windows of the apartment in the distance and said:

" 'My old aunt lives up there.' "

"And I suspect you went on to say that you were hoping for a nice little legacy from that quarter in the not-too-distant future."

"I can just hear him feeding you lies like that. All I said was that she had had two husbands and was very comfortably off.

"So he's in Toulon now. . . . He never stopped talking about Toulon and all the friends he had there."

"Do you know anything about his family?"

"No."

"Did he ever talk about his childhood?"

"No. All I know is that his mother is still alive, and that she lives in some small town in central France."

"Are you quite certain you never came here at any time during the past week or two?"

"Not again, please!"

"Think before answering."

"I'm quite sure."

"Do you know what your aunt kept in her bedside-table drawer?"

"I've never looked."

"Not even this morning, when you were rearranging the furniture for the laying out of the body?"

"Not even then."

"Did you know that your aunt had a gun?"

"Of course not! She wouldn't have dared even to pick one up."

"Wasn't she nervous, living by herself as she did?"

"She was afraid of nothing and no one."

"Did she ever talk about her second husband's inventions?"

"She showed me a little potato peeler once. She promised me one like it, actually, but I never got it. That was while Antoine was still alive. She showed me his workshop, too, if you can call it that. It's hardly bigger than a cupboard, and there isn't room to swing a cat."

"That's all. Thank you."

"Will you be at the funeral?"

"If I can manage to get there."

"The hearse will be leaving here at a quarter to ten, arriving at the church at ten."

"Till tomorrow, then."

She was tough, all right, but at times he could almost forgive her her brusque manner. Perhaps it was only the bluntness of plain speaking. She had never been attractive and had coarsened with advancing years.

She behaved more like a man than a woman, taking lovers when the whim took her. Was that really so very reprehensible?

She was quite open about it. When she felt like it, she had a man in to stay for a night or a week. The concierge had seen them come and go. The neighbors, too, must have realized what was going on.

On the other hand, she was very much on her guard, watching Maigret intently, always suspecting a trap.

On his way back to the Quai des Orfèvres, Maigret stopped at the Brasserie Dauphine for a glass of white wine from the Loire. He didn't feel like beer. The white wine in the frosted glass, with just a hint of a sparkle, seemed more appropriate on this lovely spring day.

It was the slackest time of the day. Except for a delivery man in a blue apron, there was no one in the café.

He decided to order another.

Doctor Pardon would never know. Besides, Pardon had done no more than warn him against excess.

Lapointe was waiting for him at the Quai des Orfèvres.

He had once again combed the apartments from top to bottom, showing the photograph of Le Grand Marcel to all the tenants.

"Any luck?"

"None at all."

"I'll need you tomorrow morning to drive me to the funeral."

He walked home, going over the old ground in his head. It was all very discouraging.

"The only thing we know for certain is that a revolver has disappeared."

But were they really sure even of that? They had found gun grease on the lining paper of a drawer. Might it not have got there in some other way?

Moers's men had stated positively that it had not been there for more than a month at most.

He was beginning to distrust everyone, himself included. If only he could find a new lead, however slender, he was ready to go back and start all over again, right from the beginning.

"You're early!"

For once she had not been waiting for him in the doorway, and he had had to use his key, which he very seldom did.

"I shall probably be going out later."

"Where to?"

"To a place where I think I'd better not take you, a little hippie bistro on Place Maubert."

He read slowly through the newspaper and took a shower before dinner. As on the previous evening, they dined at the table drawn up under the open window.

"Tomorrow I shall be going to the funeral."

"Will there be many people?"

"Apart from the niece, I may well be the only one. Only two of her neighbors bothered to go to pay their last respects."

"What about the press?"

"This case hasn't made the headlines. It rates only a small paragraph on page three of this evening's paper."

He switched on the television. It would be ten, at the earliest, before he could hope to find Billy Louette at the Bongo.

On the corner of Boulevard Voltaire, he hailed a taxi. The driver looked at him curiously when he gave the address, amazed that a thoroughly respectable-looking man from a district like this would go to such a disreputable dive.

The place had been decorated with the minimum of expense. The walls were painted white, with a few meaningless squiggles of color splashed on here and there.

This was the only attempt at originality. The bar was an ordinary zinc counter, with the proprietor, in shirt sleeves and a blue apron, serving behind it himself. An open door at the back led into a smoke-filled kitchen, from which came a stench of rancid fat.

There were ten or a dozen couples having dinner, which consisted mainly of spaghetti, this apparently being the specialty of the house.

Some of the younger people were in jeans and flowered shirts, but it was not these whom the crowds came to see.

To see, and, above all, to hear, because the group, which consisted of three players, was making as much noise as a full orchestra. Besides Billy and his guitar, there were a saxophone and drums.

101

All three of them had long hair and were wearing black corduroy trousers and pink shirts.

"Do you wish to order dinner?"

The proprietor had to shout to be heard at all.

Maigret shook his head and ordered white wine. Billy, who had seen him come in, seemed to take his presence there quite as a matter of course.

The Chief Superintendent knew nothing whatever about pop music, but, as far as he could tell, the Beastly Buggers were no worse than many of the groups regularly to be heard on radio and television. The three young men went at it with great verve, building up to a positively frenetic climax.

They were loudly applauded. An intermission followed, during which Billy joined Maigret at the bar.

"I take it it's me you've come to see?"

"Naturally. Have you heard from your mother?"

"Not today."

"In that case, you don't know that the funeral is fixed for tomorrow morning. Leaving the Quai de la Mégisserie at a quarter to ten. The memorial service will be held at Notre-Dame-des-Blancs-Manteaux, and the burial at the Montparnasse cemetery."

"Great-Uncle Antoine was buried at Ivry, I seem to remember."

"So he was, but your aunt expressed a wish to be buried beside her first husband."

"We'll be playing again in a few minutes. How do we sound to you?"

"I'm sorry to say I'm no judge. There's just one thing I wanted to ask you. Do you happen to know if your aunt had a revolver?"

"Yes, she did."

At last, a straight answer to a straight question!

"Did she tell you herself?"

"It was quite some time ago, at least a year or two. I didn't have a bean. I'd been to see her in the hope of making a touch, and I'd noticed that she kept several hundred-franc notes in the chest of drawers.

"A hundred francs is nothing to some people, but to others, including myself at times, it's a fortune.

"I remarked quite casually:

" 'Don't you feel nervous?'

" 'Who is there to be afraid of? You?'

" 'No. But you live alone, and people know it. Someone might break in. . . .' "

He broke off to mouth a message to his companions that he would not keep them waiting much longer.

"She said she had taken precautions against that, and she took me into her bedroom and opened her bedside-table drawer.

" 'And don't think for one moment I'd hesitate to use it.' "

Now there was something more to go on than a grease stain. Someone had actually seen the gun.

"Was it a revolver or an automatic?"

"What's the difference?"

"A revolver has a barrel. An automatic is flat."

"In that case, as far as I can remember, it was a revolver."

"How big?"

"I really couldn't say. I just had a glimpse of it. About the size of my hand, I'd say."

"Did you mention it to anyone?"

"No, not a soul."

"Not even your mother?"

"I'm not in the habit of running to her with every bit of gossip. We're not that close."

The young man returned to his companions, and the music started again. He seemed genuinely carried away by the rhythm of his guitar, counterpointed by the beat of the drums.

"He's a good kid," remarked the proprietor, leaning across the bar counter. "They're decent kids, on the whole. Not one of them touches drugs, which is more than I can say for some of my customers."

Maigret paid for his drink and went out. He had some difficulty in finding a taxi to take him home.

Next morning he went upstairs to the Examining Magistrates' floor and knocked on Judge Libart's door.

"I'd be grateful if you'd make out a search warrant for me, in the name of Angèle Louette, single. Occupation: Masseuse. Address: Rue Saint-André-des-Arts."

The clerk wrote out the warrant.

"Does this mean you'll be making an early arrest?"

"To tell you the truth, I haven't the slightest idea. I'm groping in the dark."

"Isn't she the old lady's niece?"

"Yes."

"And her sole heir? I must say that does seem rather surprising."

This, Maigret had anticipated. One's first reaction was to be one of skepticism. Angèle Louette was secure in the knowledge that sooner or later—and in view of her aunt's great age, it would probably be sooner—she would inherit the old lady's money. Why, then, should she risk life imprisonment for the sake of a legacy that was as good as hers already?

"Oh, well, never mind. You must do as you think fit, and the best of luck."

At a quarter to ten, Maigret, driven by Lapointe, drew up in one of the little black cars at the entrance to the apartment house on the Quai de la Mégisserie. There were no black draperies over the door, and not a single interested spectator.

The hearse had just arrived, and two hefty undertaker's men were on their way upstairs to get the coffin. There were no flowers, not even a wreath. At several of the windows the curtains twitched. The concierge followed the coffin as far as the door and crossed herself.

The old man with the birds ventured out of his dark shop for a moment, to join his son on the sidewalk.

That was all.

Angèle Louette, alone, stepped into the black car provided by the undertaker. The church was deserted, except for two women waiting at the confessional. Everyone seemed in a hurry to get it over and done with, not only the undertaker's men, but the priest, too.

Maigret had sat at the back of the church, to be joined by Lapointe after he had parked the car.

"Somehow, it wasn't even sad," remarked the young inspector.

He was right. The aisle was bathed in sunlight. The door had been left open, and a babble of street noises were clearly to be heard.

Et ne nos inducat in tentationem....

Amen...

The coffin, probably lighter than most, was carried out. Less than a quarter of an hour later, they were in the Montparnasse cemetery. The small procession stopped at the end of a tree-lined avenue, and the coffin was lowered into a newly dug grave, beside a flat stone of pink marble.

"I told you no one would come," whispered the masseuse, as the old woman was being laid to rest.

She went on:

"There wasn't time to have the stone engraved. She wanted her name put next to her first husband's. The stonemasons will be attending to it next week."

She was wearing a very plain black outfit, which made her look more forbidding than ever. She looked more like a governess or a headmistress than anything else.

"We'll go back to your apartment now," murmured Maigret.

"We?"

"We, yes, that's what I said."

"What do you want from me now?"

It was even more cheerful in the cemetery than in the church, with the sunlight dancing among the leaves of the trees, and the birds singing.

"One moment. I'll have to tip all those people, I suppose. I don't need to keep the car, do I?"

"There's room for you in ours."

They forgathered at the gate. Angèle got into the back of the car. Maigret took his usual seat beside Lapointe.

"Rue Saint-André-des-Arts."

Bitterly, the old lady's niece remarked:

"I was prepared for a certain amount of gossip. There

are always people ready to talk behind one's back, and, if they have nothing to go on, to invent lies. But that the Police, in the person of Chief Superintendent Maigret, should make my life a misery . . ."

"I'm truly sorry, but I'm only doing my job."

"What possible reason could I have for sneaking into my aunt's apartment?"

"What possible reason could anyone have had?"

"Do you really think me capable of murdering an old woman?"

"I don't think anything. I'm only trying to get at the truth. Join us upstairs, Lapointe, as soon as you've parked the car."

Upstairs in the apartment, she took off her hat and gloves and the jacket of her suit, under which she was wearing a white blouse. For the first time, Maigret noticed that, in spite of her mannish appearance, she had quite a good figure and was astonishingly well preserved for her age.

"Now, will you kindly tell me, once and for all, what you want from me?"

He took the Examining Magistrate's warrant out of his pocket.

"Read it for yourself."

"Does this mean that you're going to rummage through my things and turn everything upside down?"

"There's no fear of that. We know our job. Two experts from Criminal Records will be here shortly, and they will see that everything is put back exactly as it was."

"I still don't understand."

"I noticed that your son wasn't at the funeral."

"I must admit that, after everything that happened yesterday, I forgot to let him know. I haven't even got his exact address. I know only what you told me."

"You didn't let him know, but I did, which is why I was surprised not to see him there. He struck me as a responsible boy."

"Provided he always gets his own way."

"And provided no one tries to make an orthopedist of him."

"He told you about that, did he?"

"He was a great deal more co-operative than you are, and I didn't have to ask him the same questions ten times before getting straight answers...."

"He hasn't had to go through what I've been through! I don't know about you, but I need a drink."

It was not wine she needed, apparently, but whisky, which she got from a cupboard in the living room, crammed with bottles of various sorts.

"Will you join me? Or would you prefer a glass of wine? Red? White?"

"Nothing for the moment, thanks."

The men from Criminal Records arrived before Lapointe, who, no doubt, had had to go miles to find a parking place.

"All right, men, you'd better get started. Everything must be gone through with a fine-tooth comb. You know what we're looking for, but you may find something else of interest, too. All I ask is that you put everything back, exactly as you found it."

She lit a cigarette and went to sit in an armchair near the window, which commanded an extensive view of the rooftops of Paris, and from which a corner of the Eiffel Tower could also be seen.

When Lapointe finally arrived, Maigret said:

"You stay here with them. I have another call to make in the district."

Once out in the street, he made off in the direction of the Rue Mouffetard, but not until he had gulped down a glass of white wine, in a little local bistro, with a bowl of hard-boiled eggs on the bar counter.

Chapter 5

The hotel was tall and narrow and permeated with a mixture of pungent smells. Maigret, having inquired at the desk and received a grudging answer, went up to the fourth floor and knocked at the appropriate door.

A sleepy voice called out:

"Come in."

The shutters were closed, and the room was in darkness.

"I thought it must be you."

The redhead got out of bed, stark naked, and hastily tied a towel around his middle. In the bed, Maigret could just make out the contours of a girl. She was lying with her face to the wall, and all that could be seen distinctly was her dark hair spread out on the pillow.

"What time is it?"

"Much too late for you to attend the funeral."

"I suppose you want to know why I wasn't there. Hang on a minute, while I wash out my mouth. It feels like the bottom of a bird cage."

He filled the tooth mug under the running faucet and rinsed his mouth.

"It's a pity you left so early last night. You missed all the action. It was out of sight. Three guys from England turned up with their guitars, and we all got together and improvised for two hours or more. And they had a great chick with them. That's her over there.

"I just didn't have the courage to get up this morning, to go to the old girl's funeral. I feel very badly about it, but, to tell you the truth, I wasn't wild to meet my mother

"By the way, did she get hold of the loot yet?"

"What loot?"

"My great-aunt's savings. She must have had quite a nest egg. She spent almost nothing on herself. And her second husband was a saver, too. It looks as though my mother will soon get the little house she's always longed for."

He opened the shutters a crack, letting a strip of sunlight into the room. The girl groaned and turned over, revealing a naked breast.

"Was your mother planning to buy a house?"

"A small house in the country, to use on weekends at first, and eventually to retire to. She's dreamt of nothing else for years. She tried to get the old girl to lend her the money, but it didn't work out. I'm sorry I can't offer you anything."

"I just happened to be passing by."

"Have you found the revolver yet?"

"No. By the way, Le Grand Marcel has taken off."

"You don't say! My mother must be fuming!"

"She was the one who showed him the door. He's gone to Toulon, where he has friends."

"She'll need to find someone else. I doubt if she could get along for three days without a man. Unless she takes to the bottle again—but that has its problems, and it's a lot more expensive."

There was no malice in his cynicism. Indeed, there was a sort of wistfulness about him, perhaps because of the family life he had never known.

So he covered it up with a swagger.

"Don't leave Paris without letting me know. I'm nowhere near the end of this case, and I may still need your help."

The young man jerked his chin toward the bed.

"As you see, I have plenty to keep me occupied here."

Maigret returned to the Rue Saint-André-des-Arts. The men from Criminal Records were still there, waiting for him.

"We're through here, Chief. There's nothing much to report. Clothes, mostly in dark colors, underwear, stockings, and shoes. She must have a thing about shoes, because we found no less than eight pairs."

Angèle Louette was still sitting in the armchair by the window. She appeared completely unmoved.

"The refrigerator is well stocked. For a woman living by herself, she does very well. Photographs, mainly photographs of herself, when much younger, and a little boy. An account book recording the names of clients and payments received."

"You've forgotten the most important thing," broke in the second man.

The other man shrugged.

"For what it's worth! The top of the wardrobe is very

dusty, and, mixed in with the dust, we found particles of oil or grease, almost certainly gun grease."

Angèle interrupted:

"There's never been a gun in this apartment."

"Be that as it may, it's fresh grease. In the kitchen garbage can, I found some grease-stained paper, which had been used as wrapping for a revolver."

"If so, it must have been Marcel's, and no doubt he took it with him."

Maigret climbed onto a chair to see the stain for himself.

"I'd be obliged if you would come to the Quai des Orfèvres at three o'clock this afternoon."

"What about my appointments? I'm a professional woman, not a lady of leisure."

"I'm afraid I shall have to make it an official summons."

He took a yellow form from his pocket and filled in the details.

"I said three o'clock, remember."

Lapointe had been waiting patiently. They walked together to the little black car, which was parked some way off. Moers's men left at the same time.

"Is she on the telephone?"

"Yes."

"She was probably waiting only to get rid of us before ringing Toulon. Among the photographs, were there any of the old lady?"

"Three or four, taken a long time ago. There were also several of a man with a mustache, who, she said, was old Antoine."

Maigret went home to lunch. His wife was still being

tactful. She asked no questions, except about the funeral.

"Were there many people?"

"No one except the niece and ourselves, Lapointe and me. The prayers were gabbled at top speed. You'd have thought they couldn't get rid of her fast enough."

When he got back to his office, Janvier was waiting for him with a message.

"Superintendent Marella has phoned from Toulon. He wants you to call him back."

"Get him for me, will you?"

A few minutes later, he was through to him.

"Marella?"

"Yes. I called on the off-chance of finding you in. Your friend Marcel got here late last night and made straight for the Bar de l'Amiral. He spotted me at once and said, 'Good evening,' before taking a seat at the bar. He and Bob had their heads together for some time, but I couldn't hear a word they were saying, because the jukebox was going full blast."

"Was there anyone else with them?"

"No. At one point, Bob went and shut himself up in the telephone booth and made a call. He seemed very pleased with himself when he came back, and gave Marcel the thumbs-up sign."

"Was that all?"

"No. Marcel has booked himself at the Hôtel des Cinq Continents, on the Avenue de la République. He was up at nine this morning and set off by car for Sanary. Does that ring a bell?"

"No."

"It's where Pepito, the elder of the Giovanni brothers, lives."

For years the Giovannis had been responsible for most of the crime on the Riviera. Marco, the youngest of the two, lived near Paris. Pepito had built himself a luxury villa at Sanary and now lived there quietly in retirement.

They had been arrested ten or a dozen times, but there had never been enough evidence to make the charges stick.

Now that they were getting on in years, they lived the life of rich, elderly, retired gentlemen.

"How long did Marcel stay at the villa?"

"Nearly an hour. Afterward he went back to l'Amiral, and then he had lunch at an Italian restaurant in the old town."

"Did he have any previous connection with the Giovannis?"

"Not that I know of."

"Better have Pepito watched. I'd like to know where, if anywhere, he goes in the next day or two, and also whether any of his old associates start turning up at the villa."

"I'll see to it. I guess you'll do as much for me someday. How's your case going?"

"I'm beginning to see a bit of light, but there's a long way to go yet. When it's over, I've half a mind to get away for a change of scene and a bit of sun. I might even look you up."

"I'd be delighted. How long is it since we last met?"

"Ten years? Twelve years? It was over that business at Porquerolles."

"I remember. So long, Maigret."

They had signed up together at the Quai des Orfèvres and for more than two years had pounded the same beat until their promotions, after which they had first patroled the railway stations and then been assigned to detective work in the large department stores. They had both been young bachelors then.

Old Joseph came to the door, bearing the summons that Maigret had served on Angèle earlier in the day.

"Bring her in."

She was paler and more tense than usual. Perhaps she was just overawed by the portentous atmosphere of Police Headquarters.

"Take a seat."

He pointed to a straight-backed chair facing his desk and opened the door to the inspectors' duty room.

"Come in, will you, Lapointe, and bring your shorthand pad."

Young Lapointe often did duty as a stenographer. He sat down at one end of the desk, with pencil poised.

"As you see, you have been summoned here for an official interrogation. Everything you say will be taken down, and, at the end, you will be required to read and sign the transcript. I may have to repeat some questions that I have already put to you, but this time your answers will be on record."

"In other words, I'm suspect number one, is that it?"

"You're a suspect, that's all. Numbers don't come into it.

"You hadn't the slightest affection for your aunt. Isn't that so?"

"When I told her I was pregnant, the best she could do for me was to hand me a hundred-franc note."

"And you resented what you regarded as her meanness?"

"She was thoroughly selfish. She never gave a thought to others. And I'm quite sure in my own mind that the only reason she married again was because there was money in it."

"Was she a deprived child?"

"She didn't even have that excuse. Her father was a man of property, as they used to say. The family lived near the Luxembourg Gardens, and the two girls, my mother and my aunt, went to a very good school. It wasn't until my grandfather was well advanced in years that he began to speculate recklessly, and eventually lost all he possessed."

"Was it then that she married Caramé?"

"Yes. He was a frequent visitor at my grandparents'. Everyone thought at first that it was my mother he was interested in. I imagine she thought so, too. But it was my aunt who got him in the end."

"And your mother?"

"She married a bank clerk. He was in poor health, and he died young. She went to work for a business firm in the Rue Paradis."

"So life was none too easy for the two of you?"

"That's right."

"Didn't your aunt offer to help?"

"No. I don't quite know what made me decide to become a masseuse. Unless it was that one of our neighbors was a masseuse, and I used to see her drive off in her car to visit her clients."

"Do you have a car?"

"A small one."

"To drive to your country house, when you get it?"

She frowned.

"Who told you that?"

"Never mind. I gather you've always had this dream of

owning a little house, not too far out of town, where you could go on weekends."

"Well, what's wrong with that? It's what lots of people want. It was my mother's dearest wish, too, only she died before it came true."

"How much do you hope to get from your aunt's estate?"

"Forty to fifty thousand francs, perhaps. I don't know. I'm only going on what she told me. She may have had other investments that she didn't mention."

"In other words, you went on seeing her because of what you were hoping to get?"

"You can put it that way if you like. But don't forget, she was my only living relative. Have you ever had to live alone, Monsieur Maigret?"

"What about your son?"

"I hardly ever see him, except when he's broke. I mean nothing to him."

"Before I put my next question to you, I must remind you that everything you say is put on record, and urge you to think carefully before you speak. Did you often go to your aunt's apartment while she was out?"

It seemed to him that she had turned a shade paler, but her self-possession was unshaken.

"Do you mind if I smoke?"

"Please do, but I'm afraid I haven't any cigarettes to offer you."

On his desk there were pipes only, six pipes arranged in sizes, side by side in a rack.

"I asked you a question."

"I'd be grateful if you would repeat it."

He did so, slowly and clearly, and without hesitation.

"It depends on what you mean by going to her apartment. Sometimes I called at the Quai de la Mégisserie and found her out. On those occasions I waited until she got back."

"In the apartment?"

"No. Outside, on the landing."

"Did you often have to wait for a long time?"

"When she was a long time coming, I used to go for a walk along the Quai or, more often, just look at the birds."

"Didn't it ever occur to your aunt to give you a key to the apartment?"

"No."

"Suppose she had been taken ill suddenly?"

"She'd made up her mind that it couldn't happen to her. She never had so much as a fainting fit in the whole of her life."

"Did she ever leave the door open?"

"No."

"Not even when she was at home?"

"No. She always took good care to see that it was shut."

"Was there someone in particular she didn't trust?"

"She didn't trust anyone."

"Not even you?"

"I don't know."

"Was her manner toward you affectionate?"

"It was completely matter-of-fact. She'd tell me to sit down. Then she'd make me coffee and serve it to me with some dry biscuits out of a tin."

"Did she ever ask about your son?"

"No. I imagine she saw him quite as often as I did, if not more."

"Did she ever threaten to disinherit you?"

"Why should she do that?"

"To get back to the front door, I've had a look at the lock. There's nothing very special about it. Anyone could have taken a wax impression of it."

"What for?"

"Never mind. Allow me to put my question another way: were you ever, on any occasion, alone in the apartment?"

"Never."

"Think carefully."

"I have thought very carefully."

"Didn't it ever happen that, while you were there, your aunt had to go out to get something from the shops, such as a fresh supply of biscuits, for instance?"

"No."

"So you never got a chance to go through her drawers?"

"No."

"And you never saw her Post Office Savings book?"

"I caught a glimpse of it once, when she was getting something out of the drawer, but I don't know what was in it."

"What about her bankbook?"

"I haven't the slightest idea how much she had in the bank. As a matter of fact, I didn't even know she had a bank account."

"But you knew she had money?"

"I was pretty sure of it."

"I don't mean just her savings."

"I don't know what you're talking about. What do you mean?"

"Never mind. Did you ever try to borrow money from her?"

"Just the once, as I told you. That time when I was pregnant, and she gave me a hundred francs."

"More recently than that, I mean. You wanted to buy a country cottage. Did you ever ask her to help you toward that?"

"No. You don't know what she was like."

"I did meet her."

"And you were taken in, just like everyone else. You took her for a sweet old lady, with a gentle smile and a shy manner, whereas, in actual fact, she was as hard as nails."

"Do you own a red-striped or red-check scarf?"

"No."

"Do you remember the red-striped cushion on the couch in your aunt's sitting room?"

"Vaguely, yes, I think I do."

"You had a quarrel with your friend Marcel yesterday morning. What was that about?"

"He was becoming impossible."

"What do you mean by that?"

"Naturally, when I take up with a man, I don't ask for references. But Marcel went too far. He didn't even bother to look for work. He could have got a job as a barman ten times over. But he preferred to sponge off me."

"Did he know your aunt?"

"I'd hardly be likely to introduce him to her, would I?"

"Did he know of her existence?"

"I may have mentioned her."

"And told him, no doubt, that she had a nice little nest egg tucked away?"

"I would hardly have put it quite like that."

"Be that as it may, he knew where she lived and that, to say the least, she had a considerable sum put away."

"Yes, I suppose he did."

"Did you ever see him going into the house on the Quai de la Mégisserie?"

"Never."

"And yet there are at least two witnesses who saw him there."

"Well, it's more than I ever did."

"Did you ever consider marrying him?"

"Certainly not. Since my son was born, I've never once thought of marriage. I get what I want from a man when I want it, and that's all there is to it. Do I make myself clear?"

"Perfectly. Now, about the revolver."

"What, again?"

"It must be somewhere, and I'm determined to find it. For some considerable time, your aunt kept it in the drawer of her bedside table. According to you, your aunt was terrified of firearms, and you find it hard to believe that she ever owned a gun."

"That's right."

"Nevertheless, she did own a gun, and she always kept it handy, which, incidentally, rather suggests that she was more concerned for her safety than you led me to suppose."

"What's all this leading up to?"

Maigret, with great deliberation, refilled his pipe.

"This morning, at your apartment, we found evidence

that your aunt's gun had, at some time, been concealed on top of your wardrobe."

"That's what you say."

"I'm having tests done to confirm it. One of two people must have put the gun there: you or your lover."

"I object to that term."

"Does it embarrass you?"

"It's inaccurate. There was no love in our relationship."

"Let's suppose, for the sake of argument, that he did go to the Quai de la Mégisserie."

"To murder my aunt?"

"To look for her nice little nest egg, to use the expression you objected to just now. The old lady came back and found herself face to face with him. And he snatched up a cushion from the couch and smothered her with it."

"Where does the revolver come into it? Why should he have taken it? Why should he have hidden it on top of my wardrobe, and why, when he left for Toulon, should he have taken it with him?"

"So you think he took it with him?"

"If it really exists, it must, as you say yourself, be somewhere. As to myself, I assure you that I was nowhere near my aunt's apartment on the afternoon of her death. And I don't believe for a moment that Marcel was, either. He may be a bad sort, as they say, but he's not a killer. Any more questions?"

"Have you done anything about claiming your inheritance?"

"Not yet. I have an appointment later today with an attorney, the husband of one of my clients. If it hadn't been for him, I wouldn't have known where to turn."

She stood up, with every appearance of relief.

"When will you want my signature?"

"On your statement, do you mean? How long will it take you to type it, Lapointe?"

"It'll be ready in half an hour."

"In half an hour. I suggest you make yourself comfortable in the waiting room, meanwhile."

"Can't I come back some other time?"

"No, I want to get it over and done with. You can see your lawyer later, and by tonight you'll be some tens of thousands of francs the richer. Incidentally, do you intend to move into your aunt's apartment?"

"No. My own suits me perfectly well."

Holding herself stiffly erect, she went to the door and, without another word, left the room.

He caught the night train and was fortunate enough to get a sleeping compartment to himself. He awoke at dawn, as he always did when traveling south, just as the train drew into Montélimar.

To him, Montélimar had always been the frontier town of Provence. From there on, he couldn't bear to miss an inch of the landscape. He loved everything about it, the trees and flowers, the countryside, the pale-pink and lavender-blue houses, with their sun-baked tiled roofs, the villages with their avenues of plane trees and their little bars, where people were already gathering.

At Marseilles, while the train was shunting in the Gare Saint-Charles, he listened with relish to the lilt in the voices of the people.

It was a long time since he and his wife had last been to the Riviera. Why shouldn't they spent their next vacation there? But it would be the height of the season by then, and the whole area would be swarming with tourists.

A few more miles and there was the sea, as blue as in any postcard, dotted with boats, with motionless fishermen aboard.

Superintendent Marella was waiting for him on the station platform, and waving enthusiastically.

"Why don't you come more often? How many years is it since you were last in Toulon?"

"About ten, as I told you on the telephone. I hope you don't mind my trespassing on your territory like this."

Maigret was outside his bailiwick. Here Marella was the boss. Needless to say, he was dark-haired, not exactly tall but extremely ebullient. Since their last meeting, he had developed something of a paunch, which somehow lent him an air of respectability.

In the old days, he had looked more like a gangster than a police officer. Gangsters are no less prone to middle-aged spread than the rest of us, but they usually retire before it overtakes them.

"Would you care for a coffee?"

"I'd love one. I had a cup on the train, but it was wretched."

"All right, then, let's go. There's a decent little place across the square."

The square was shimmering in the heat. They went into a café-restaurant and sat down at the bar.

"Come on, then. Tell me all about it."

"There's nothing to tell. It's a queer business. I can't make any sense of it. I'm just floundering. Where is Marcel at the moment?"

"In bed. He spent half the night whooping it up with

his buddies at the Restaurant Victor, opposite the Port-Marchand. They're a bunch of crooks. Later they were joined by some girls."

"Did you ever come across him when he lived here?"

"He was never in Toulon for very long. His longest stay was two years. I should tell you that none of the crooks hereabouts takes him very seriously. He's looked on as a bit of an amateur."

"Who's this fellow Bob, whom he uses as an accommodation address?"

"The barman at l'Amiral. He's up to every trick. At any rate, none of us here has ever been able to pin anything on him."

"And the Giovanni brothers?"

"Only one of them lives here, Pepito, the older of the two. The other, I'm told, has a place just outside Paris. Pepito owns a magnificent villa, which he bought from a rich old American who decided she wanted to go home and lay her bones in the old country. It's the finest property in Sanary, with its own private anchorage, in which he keeps his motor launch.

"He's practically a recluse and scarcely ever sees any of his old cronies. 'Out of sight, out of mind' appears to be his motto. Even so, I've been keeping an eye on him. And, what's more, he knows it, and whenever we pass in the street, he greets me most cordially."

"I wonder what on earth Marcel could possibly have had to say to him."

"Me, too. Especially since Marcel was never one of his boys."

"Where is he staying?"

"At the Hôtel des Cinq Continents, on the Avenue de la République. It's almost next door to the Harbormaster's Office."

It was only eight o'clock.

"Would you mind coming with me? It will help put you in the picture. He'll probably be livid at being waked up at this time of the morning."

Maigret did not book into a hotel, since he was hoping to be able to leave that same evening. Marella inquired at the desk for the number of Marcel's room, and they went up together and knocked loudly on his door. It was some time before a sleepy voice called out:

"Who's there?"

"Police."

It was Marella who had spoken. Marcel, in crumpled pajamas and barefooted, stumbled to the door and opened it.

"Christ! Not you again!" he grumbled, catching sight of Maigret. "Oh, well, since you're with Superintendent Marella . . ."

He pulled back the curtains, lit a cigarette, and hastily removed a pair of trousers, which had been thrown on a chair.

"What have I done now?" he asked.

"Nothing new, as far as I know."

"As a matter of fact," broke in Marella, addressing Marcel, "there was one thing. Yesterday afternoon you went to see Handsome Maria. Don't you know that, for months now, she's been Scarface's girl?"

"I also know that he's in the clink."

"True enough. I brought him in last week, and this

time it's on a very serious charge: trafficking in drugs, no less. All the same, he's got friends on the outside, and you're not in your territory here."

"Thanks for the tip. But she's a very old friend. But what about you, Monsieur Maigret? What brings you all this way, only two days after our last meeting?"

"Maybe I've come to take you back to Paris."

"What? You must be joking!"

"First of all, there's that little matter of the key."

"What key?"

"The key to the old lady's apartment. Who took the wax impression? Angèle couldn't have managed that by herself."

Marcel didn't bat an eyelid.

"All right! Save your answers for your official statement, which will be taken down, and which you will be required to sign."

"For Chrissake, don't you ever listen? I know nothing whatever about that dirty business, I tell you! Okay, I was living with the Sergeant-Major, though only, I might say, until I found something better, and I was only too glad to be rid of her."

"There are at least two witnesses who remember seeing you."

"How did they identify me?"

"From a photograph in our files, or rather in the Vice Squad's files."

"And who are these two witnesses?"

"The owner of the pet shop on the ground floor and the tenant who lives in the apartment across the landing from the old lady. You actually bumped into her on the stairs, because you weren't looking where you were going, and you apologized."

"They must both be mad."

"You were wearing the same check suit that you had on the day before yesterday."

"I bought it in one of the big department stores. There must be thousands like it in Paris."

"So, you had no key. Did you pick the lock?"

"How much longer is this going to go on?"

"I couldn't say. Why?"

"Because, if you intend to stay, I'd like to order myself some breakfast."

"Go ahead."

He rang for the floor waiter and ordered coffee and *croissants.*

"And if you were expecting me to order something for you, you're in for a disappointment. I've never picked a lock in my life. I wouldn't know how."

"When did she first tell you about the revolver?"

"Who?"

"You know very well who. Angèle. You're not suggesting, are you, that you guessed the old lady kept a revolver in her apartment?"

"I didn't even know of the old girl's existence."

"That's a lie. Angèle has admitted, in her signed statement, that she pointed to the windows of her aunt's apartment and told you that she was her heir."

"And you believe her? She'd lie as soon as look at you, that one."

"And you wouldn't, I suppose?"

"I'm telling you the truth. You won't trip me up,

just because you've got your nasty, suspicious eye on me. Take that photograph you got from the Vice Squad. When was it taken, I'd like to know? I have no recollection of it."

The waiter came in with the coffee and *croissants*, which filled the room with an appetizing smell. He put the tray down on a small pedestal table. Marcel, still in his pajamas and barefooted, drew up a chair and began to eat.

Marella glanced at Maigret with eyebrows raised, as though seeking permission to intervene.

"What were you and Bob talking about?"

"The night before last, soon after I got here? I told him all my news, and he told me his. We're old friends, and it's been a long time since we last met."

"And what else?"

"I don't know what you mean."

"Which of the two of you thought of Giovanni?"

"I think I did. I knew him, too, back in the old days, when he lived in Montmartre. I was only a kid then."

"Why, in that case, didn't you call him yourself?"

"What for?"

"To make an appointment to see him. As Bob did on your behalf. What was it you wanted to talk to him about?"

"I don't know what you're talking about."

"Don't be an idiot. As you very well know, you can't just turn up on Giovanni's doorstep, especially if you happen to be nothing more than a low-down, broke little pimp. But the fact remains that you did go to see him yesterday, and you were with him for nearly an hour."

"I just went for a chat, that's all."

"And what, may I ask, did you chat about?"

Marcel was beginning to show signs of nervousness. He was not at all happy with this particular line of inquiry.

"Let's say I went to ask him for a job. He has a great many irons in the fire, all on the level. I thought he could probably use a man he could trust."

"Did he hire you?"

"He wanted time to think it over. He said he'd let me know in a day or two."

Once more Marella glanced at Maigret, to indicate that he had finished.

"You heard what my colleague, Marella, said just now. He will be giving the necessary instructions to his staff. You will therefore oblige us by coming to his office and repeating all you have said to us. This will be taken down by a stenographer, and, in due course, you will be required to sign the transcript.

"Be sure you leave nothing out, especially where Bob and Giovanni are concerned."

"Do I have to bring him into it?"

"Have you told the truth?"

"Yes. But he wouldn't like it if he knew I'd been discussing him with the cops."

"I'm afraid you have no choice. And don't try to leave Toulon until we give you the word."

"Whatever you say, but if I don't manage to find a job, will you pay my hotel bill?"

"Maybe we can arrange to put you up somewhere else," interposed Marella. "It's nice and cool in there, at any rate."

The two men went out into the street.

"I hope you didn't think I was presuming?" said Marella, a little anxiously.

"Not at all. You were most helpful. I'd appreciate it if you'd do the same for me with Bob."

The Bar de l'Amiral was just on the other side of the street, on the corner of the quai and a narrow dead end. Out on the sidewalk were four tables, covered with cloths of a small check pattern. In the open, the sunshine, reflected on the shimmering expanse of water, was dazzling. In contrast, the interior of the bar was dark and pleasantly cool.

A barman, with the broken nose and cauliflower ears of a boxer, was busy washing glasses. It was too early in the day for customers, and the room was deserted except for a waiter who was setting the tables.

"Good morning, Superintendent. What can I get you?"

He spoke to Marella, whom he knew. Maigret was a stranger to him.

"Do you have a good local wine?" asked Maigret.

"A carafe of *rosé?*"

"Two glasses, or a carafe, as you wish."

Both men were relaxed. Only Bob appeared uneasy.

"You had a visitor last night, I noticed, Bob."

"We're never short of visitors here, you know."

"I don't mean a customer. I'm referring to someone who came all the way from Paris just to see you."

"To see me, me in particular?"

"Well, let's say, to ask you a favor."

"I can't imagine what."

"Have you known him long?"

"Seven or eight years."

"Is he on the level?"

"He's never done time, if that's what you mean. He hasn't got a record."

"And what about you?"

"You know the answer to that. I haven't got a perfectly clean sheet."

"What did he want?"

"He happened to be passing by, and he just dropped in for a chat."

"He asked you to make a telephone call for him."

"Oh?"

"Don't play the fool with me. One of my men was in here at the time. You left your friend at the bar and shut yourself up in the telephone booth to make a call. It was a long call. Your friend was very jumpy. When you got back, you talked to him at some length in an undertone, after which he looked a good deal relieved."

"Maybe it was about his ex-girlfriend, Maria. He'd been to see her."

"Is she living at Sanary now?"

"You must be joking!"

"It's not in your interest to hold out on me, Bob. The person you spoke to on the telephone was Pepito Giovanni. You worked for him once, before he went straight. You persuaded him to see Marcel. Quite a feat, because Giovanni won't see any Tom, Dick, or Harry, especially in his own house. How did you manage it?"

"I just told Giovanni that I had a friend with me who was looking for a job."

"No!"

"Why do you say no?"

"Because you know as well as I do that it's not true. Giovanni will laugh his head off when I tell him."

"I told him that Marcel had an interesting proposition to put to him. And nothing illegal about it, either."

"Did he show you the model?"

"No."

"Do you know what it is?"

"Marcel didn't tell me. All he would say was that it was something very, very big, with international potential, and likely to be of special interest to the Americans."

"That's a bit more like it. Maybe we're getting to the truth at last. Was Giovanni interested?"

"He agreed to see Marcel yesterday afternoon at three."

"Anything else?"

"He said to be sure and see that no one went with him, and to tell him not to forget the model."

The *vin rosé* was fruity in flavor and perfectly chilled. Maigret listened to the interchange, smiling a little to himself. He had always had a great affection for his colleague, and it occurred to him that had Marella stayed in Paris, he might well now be sitting in his, Maigret's, seat at the Quai des Orfèvres. But he was more in his element in Toulon. He had been born in Nice and knew every delinquent and prostitute from Menton to Marseilles.

"Is there anything you want to ask him, Maigret?"

Bob frowned.

"Do you mean to say that's Chief Superintendent Maigret with you?"

"None other. And, if you don't watch out, he's the one you may find yourself up against."

"Forgive me, I didn't recognize you."

And, as Maigret was opening his wallet:

"No, no. It's on the house."

"I'm sorry, I can't agree to that."

He laid a ten-franc note on the table.

"I presume that the minute we've left you'll be on the phone to Giovanni?"

"Not if you don't want me to. I don't want to get on the wrong side of you. Or of Superintendent Marella, for that matter."

They stood for a moment in the sunlit square, watching the sailors go by, with their navy-blue collars and red pompons.

"Do you want me to come with you to see Giovanni? Or would you rather go alone?"

"I wouldn't dream of going without you."

"In that case, let's go back to Police Headquarters to get my car."

They drove through La Seyne-sur-Mer, where they saw a ship being taken apart, and were soon in sight of Sanary Point, on the very end of which stood an imposing villa.

"That's the house. Even if Bob has kept his word, Marcel will have been in touch with him, so he'll be expecting us. It won't be such smooth sailing with him."

Chapter 6

He came toward them, hand outstretched, across a huge living room, which was bathed in sunlight. He was wearing a cream-colored Shantung suit.

"Good day to you, Marella," he said; then, pretending to notice Maigret for the first time:

"Chief Superintendent Maigret, of all people! This is an unexpected honor."

He was a fine-looking man, powerfully built, but without an ounce of surplus fat. Maigret knew that he must be over sixty, but, at first glance at least, he looked nearer fifty.

The drawing room was furnished with great taste, probably by an interior decorator, and there was a hint of the theater about it, because of its lofty proportions.

"Where would you prefer to sit, here or on the terrace?"

He led the way out and installed them in comfortable lounging chairs under a beach umbrella.

The butler, in a white jacket, had followed them out and stood, a watchful figure, awaiting orders.

"What would you like to drink? May I suggest a Tom Collins? I know of nothing more refreshing at this time of day."

Maigret and Marella indicated their approval.

"Two Tom Collinses, Georges, and the usual for me."

He was close-shaven, with well-kept hands and manicured nails. His manner was easy and relaxed.

"Did you just get here?" he asked Maigret, by way of making polite conversation.

The terrace looked out onto the sea, which seemed to extend to infinity. A motor launch rocked gently in the little private anchorage.

"I came on the night train."

"Don't tell me you came all this way just to see me!"

"I had no idea, when I arrived, that I'd be coming to see you at all."

"Even so, I'm flattered."

Beneath his genial manner he was a hard man, however much he tried to conceal it by a display of affability.

"At any rate, you're not on home territory now, Chief Superintendent."

"True enough, but my good friend, Marella here, is."

"Marella and I are on excellent terms, aren't we, Marella?"

"Just so long as you keep on the right side of the law."

"I lead such a very quiet life, you know that. I hardly ever go out. You could almost say that my whole world is bounded by these four walls. I never see a soul, except for a friend occasionally, or a pretty girl from time to time."

"Do you number Le Grand Marcel among your friends?"

He looked shocked.

"That seedy little runt who came to see me yesterday morning?"

"Be that as it may, you did agree to see him."

"It's a point of principle with me never to refuse a helping hand. There have been times in the past when I, too, was in need of help."

"And did you help him?"

The butler reappeared with a tray, on which there were two tall frosted glasses and a smaller glass of tomato juice.

"Please forgive me. I never touch wine or spirits. Cheers!

"But I interrupted you. What was it you were saying?"

"I asked you if you had been able to help him."

"Unfortunately not. I couldn't see my way to fitting him in anywhere.

"You see, Monsieur Maigret, a lot of water has flowed under the Pont-Neuf since we last met. Nowadays, I'm a highly respected business tycoon, if I may say so.

"I own a dozen movie theaters up and down the Riviera: two in Marseilles, one in Nice, one in Antibes, and three in Cannes, not to mention the one in Aix-en-Provence.

"I am also the proprietor of a night club in Marseilles, and of three hotels, one of them in Menton.

"And all perfectly respectable, I assure you. Isn't that so, Marella?"

"Quite correct."

"I also own a restaurant in Paris, on the Avenue de la Grande-Armée. My brother manages it for me. It's an extremely smart place, and the food is superb. You'll be welcome there as my guest, any time."

Maigret was watching him closely, his expression inscrutable.

"You must see, Chief Superintendent, that in my kind of setup, there's no room for a petty little pimp like Marcel."

"Did he leave the model with you?"

Giovanni, for all his self-assurance, was visibly shaken.

"Model? What are you talking about? You must be making a mistake."

"You agreed to see Marcel because Bob told you on the telephone that he was onto something big, something with almost unlimited potential."

"I don't understand. It sounds like a fairy tale to me. Surely you didn't get it from Bob?"

"I understand that it was likely to be of particular interest to the Americans."

"But I have no American business connections."

"I'm going to tell you a little story, Giovanni, and I hope you learn something from it. Once upon a time, there lived in Paris a dear little old lady who got it into her head that someone was sneaking into her apartment while she was out, and moving her things, so that, when she got back, everything was very slightly out of place."

"I don't see what..."

"Let me finish. This same old lady came to Police Headquarters to ask for protection, but, I'm sorry to say, we all thought she was mad, to begin with at least. Still, I had intended to go to see her, if only to reassure her."

"I seem to remember reading something about it in the newspapers."

"It was referred to briefly, but the press had no idea what it was really all about."

"Would you care for a cigar?"

"Thank you, but I prefer my pipe."

"What about you, Marella?"

"With pleasure."

There was a box of Havana cigars on the table. Giovanni and Marella each took one.

"Forgive me. I shouldn't have interrupted you. You went to call on the old lady...."

"There's a lot more before we get to that."

"Please go on."

"She had an elderly niece with a marked predilection for men much younger than herself. For the past six months, for instance, she's had Marcel living with her, that same Marcel who came to see you yesterday."

Giovanni was now listening with interest.

"The old lady was murdered before I had a chance to go to see her, as I had promised."

"How was she killed?"

"She was suffocated with a cushion. She couldn't, at her age, put up very much of a fight."

"I still don't understand what all this has to do with me."

"As I told you, Le Grand Marcel and the old lady's niece were lovers. There are two witnesses who are prepared to swear that they saw him in the house where the old lady lived on at least one occasion."

"Do you suspect him of the murder?"

"Either him or the niece. It comes to the same thing, more or less."

"What were they after?"

"The model."

"What do you mean?"

"Whatever it was that Marcel came to sell you."

"And what might that be?"

"You should know better than I do, since, unless I'm very much mistaken, it is now in your possession."

"I still don't know what you're talking about."

"I'm talking about a revolver. I may as well admit right away that I don't know what sort of revolver, or what there is about it that makes it so special."

"I've never carried a gun in my life, as you very well know. Even in the early days, when I was just a young delinquent, I was often stopped and searched by the police, but they were never once able to charge me with being in illegal possession of a firearm."

"I know."

"That being so, what possible inducement do you suppose there could be for me to take a revolver from a sleazy little pimp like Marcel?"

"Don't worry. I'm not going to ask my friend Marella to rummage through your house from cellar to attic. You're far too wily a customer to leave the article in question in any place where we could hope to find it."

"You flatter me. How about another Tom Collins?"

"One is quite enough, thanks all the same."

Marella had never seen Maigret so circumspect. He spoke very quietly, as though what he was saying mattered very little, and yet, somehow, every word struck home.

"I didn't expect you to admit the real purpose of Le Grand Marcel's visit, I came simply to warn you. You certainly won't have learned from him that the revolver in question is a vital clue in a murder case.

"The murder itself was unpremeditated. The old lady, who used to spend the greater part of every afternoon sitting on a bench in the Tuileries, must, for some reason, have returned home earlier than usual. The intruder, man or woman . . ."

"Do you mean the niece?"

"The niece, yes. He or she snatched up a cushion from the couch and held it over the old lady's face for as long as was necessary.

"I'm sure I don't need to labor the point, but you must realize that any international deal you may have in mind could have damaging repercussions affecting your legitimate business interests, your hotels and restaurants and so forth."

Maigret fell silent. His expression was bland. Giovanni was looking a little uneasy, and doing his best to conceal it.

"Thanks for the warning. I can assure you that if the fellow turns up here again, he won't get past the door."

"He won't come back until you give him the word, and I know you won't do that."

"Did you know about this, Marella?"

"Not until yesterday."

"I trust you have put your colleague, Maigret here, in the picture. Does he know that I am now a highly respected businessman, and that I'm on the very best of terms with all those in authority, from the Prefect downward?"

"I did tell him, yes."

"Then it only remains for me to repeat that I am in no way involved in this sordid little affair."

Maigret stood up with a sigh.

"Thanks for the drink."

Marella also got to his feet, and the two men, accompanied by Giovanni, crossed the vast living room and stood for a moment in the doorway at the top of the broad flight of marble steps that led down to the garden.

"You'll always be welcome here, at any time, gentlemen."

They got into Marella's car.

When they were outside the main gates, Maigret said:

"There must be some little pub or other in the neighborhood from which we can see the villa. If you know of one, stop there."

They found a little bistro, painted blue, in Sanary itself. Outside there were four men playing bowls.

"What will you have?"

"A glass of *rosé*. That Tom Collins left a nasty taste in my mouth."

"I couldn't make out what you were up to," murmured Marella. "You didn't press home your advantage. I almost got the impression that you wanted him to think you believed him."

"Well, for one thing, he's not the man to give anything away."

"That's true."

"And anyway, what have I got to go on? After a telephone call from Bob the barman, he agreed to see our shady little friend. I haven't even got an accurate description of the revolver."

"So there really is a revolver?"

"There most certainly is. That was what the intruders were looking for when they disturbed the old lady's knickknacks.

"And even if you were able to spare every man you've got for the search, what hope would we have of finding it in that great barracks of a place? You don't imagine, do you, that Giovanni just slipped it into his bedside-table drawer?

"Anyway, we shall soon see whether I'm right."

And, a quarter of an hour later, they did see. A man in a yachting cap appeared, boarded the little motor launch, and started up the engine.

A few seconds later Giovanni followed him down the steps to the landing and climbed aboard.

"Don't you see, it's too hot for him to handle. He can't wait to get rid of it. At any rate, the deal is off."

The launch nosed out of the anchorage and headed for the open sea in a swath of spray.

"In a few minutes, the revolver will be heaven knows how many fathoms deep on the ocean bed. It will never be found."

"I see."

"At any rate, there's nothing more for me to do, here in Toulon."

"I hope you'll stay to dine with us. We've got a spare room now."

"I'm going back on the night train."

"Do you really have to?"

"I'm afraid so. I've got a very busy day ahead of me tomorrow."

"The niece?"

"Among others. Le Grand Marcel will still need watching, and if you take my advice, you'll keep an eye on that fellow Bob. It strikes me he has a good deal too much influence for a mere barman. Do you really believe Giovanni is as straight as he makes out?"

"I've been trying to catch him for years. Men of his

sort, even when they've bought their passport to respectability, like to keep discreetly in touch with their old buddies in the underworld. You've just seen for yourself."

The white launch, having described a wide arc in the sea, was now returning to the anchorage.

"No doubt he's feeling mighty relieved now that he's got rid of his precious model."

"What do you plan to do between now and catching your train?"

"I'd like another word with Le Grand Marcel. Do you think I might find him at Maria's?"

"I very much doubt it. After what I told him about her boy friend, he's sure to keep well away from her. He may act tough, but it's only an act. He's not the sort to stick his neck out."

"What about l'Amiral?"

"He's sure to go there sometime."

It was five o'clock by the time they got to l'Amiral. The bar, once again, was deserted, and Bob was sitting at a table with Le Grand Marcel, who, on catching sight of the two police officers, burst out:

"What, again!"

"Yes, here we are again. Would you bring us a carafe of *rosé*, Bob?"

"How many times do I have to tell you that I didn't kill the old girl?"

"Be that as it may, you did go to her apartment on the Quai de la Mégisserie."

Maigret, looking very benign, had used the familiar "*tu.*"

"I'd like to see you prove it. I'd also like you to tell me what I was supposed to be doing there."

"Looking for the model."

"I don't know what you're talking about."

"I've just come from seeing someone else who said exactly the same thing, someone a lot tougher than you are. But, in spite of what he said, he knew well enough."

"You've been to see Giovanni?"

Marcel had gone very white. Bob came up to the table with a carafe of wine and two glasses on a tray.

"What did he tell you?"

"A good prospect on the international market, did you say, and likely to be of particular interest to the Americans?"

"I still don't know what you're talking about."

"Forget it. Only, I'm warning you that if you have it in mind to go back to the villa in Sanary in the hope of making a killing, you'd better think again."

Bob, resuming his seat at the table, asked:

"Have you seen Giovanni?"

"We've just come from there."

"Did he tell you Marcel had been to see him?"

"And that you had called to make the appointment."

He savored the local wine, sipping it with discernment. In two hours' time he would be on the train, on his way back to Paris.

Then he turned his attention once more to Marcel.

"If it really wasn't you who killed the old lady, you'd be well advised to tell me the whole truth and come back with me to Paris."

Nervously, the man clenched his long fingers.

"What do you have to say about it, Bob?"

"It's none of my business, really. I'm ready to give a helping hand to a friend, when I can, but that's as far as it goes. I don't know anything about this business."

"What should I go back to Paris for?" asked Marcel.

"To get yourself safely locked up in jail."

"But I've already told you ..."

"I know, I know. You didn't kill the old lady. It was her niece who did it. That won't prevent your being charged as an accessory."

"And so you're advising me to leave Toulon, to make it easy for you to arrest me?"

"I have a feeling you'd be safer in Paris than here."

A look of cunning spread over Marcel's features.

"Oh, no, Chief Superintendent. I wasn't born yesterday. If you have a warrant for my arrest, show it to me and I'll come quietly. But, as you very well know, you can't arrest me without evidence, and all you've got is a couple of lousy witnesses who claim to have seen someone wearing a check suit like mine."

"It's up to you."

"So that's my reward for keeping my nose clean for years!"

"It's a pity you couldn't keep it up."

This time it was Marella who paid for the drinks. Then, glancing at his watch, he said:

"You'll just have time to come say hello to my wife and see our new house."

It was a little way out of the town, on a hill. It was quite a small villa, but pleasant and colorful, with a very attractive view.

A boy of about fifteen was mowing the lawn. The motor buzzed like a gigantic bluebottle.

"You know my son, Alain."

"He was a baby when I last saw him."

"As you can see, the baby has grown somewhat."

They went into the spacious living room. Madame Marella emerged from the kitchen, a rolling pin in hand.

"Oh! Sorry. I didn't realize we had a visitor."

Maigret kissed her on both cheeks. Her name was Claudine, and he had never seen her without a smile.

"You'll stay for dinner, I hope. I'm just in the middle of making a strawberry tart."

"He's got to catch the night train back to Paris."

"Have you been here long, Maigret?"

"I arrived this morning."

"Do you really have to go back so soon?"

"Thanks to your husband's invaluable help, I've done what I came to do."

"What can I give you? If I remember, you seemed to like our local wines. I've got much better stuff in the cellar than anything they stock at l'Amiral."

For nearly an hour they sat talking of this and that. Alain, the fifteen-year-old son, came in to shake the Chief Superintendent by the hand.

"Why aren't you at school?"

"It's Saturday. Did you forget?"

So it was. Maigret had forgotten. In the confusion of the past week he had lost all track of time.

"What class are you in?"

"Classical Third."

"Will you be following in your father's footsteps?"

"Oh, no! Just think of the hours! And even when you're in bed, there's no guarantee you won't be called out again. Father never knows when the telephone might ring."

Maigret felt sad. He had always longed for a son of his own, even a son who didn't want to be a policeman.

"I must be on my way. I can't miss my train."

"I'll drive you to the station."

A few minutes later they were in the car, and Claudine was waving good-bye from the top of the steps.

Boulevard Richard-Lenoir, as always on a Sunday morning, was almost deserted. The sound of a taxi door slamming was enough to bring Madame Maigret running to the window.

She was waiting for him on the landing.

"I thought you'd be spending the night in Toulon. Why didn't you call to let me know you were coming?"

"I thought I'd give you a surprise."

She was doing the housework, with her head tied up in a scarf.

"You didn't wear yourself out, I hope."

"Not in the least. I had a very good night's sleep."

"Shall I run you a bath?"

"Yes, that would be lovely."

He had shaved on the train, as he always did when returning to Paris.

"Did everything work out all right?"

"More or less. Incidentally, Marella and Claudine send you their kindest regards. They've built themselves a very pretty little house on the outskirts of town."

"Claudine was as cheerful as ever, I suppose?"

"She hasn't changed. The only one who has is their son. He's a big fellow now, with a very deep voice."

"Are you free for the rest of the day?"

"Almost, though I'll have to go out for a little while later."

While his bath was running, he called Police Headquarters. Once again it was old Lucas who was on duty.

"Has anything been happening while I've been away?"

"Nothing special, Chief."

"Who's there with you?"

"Neveu, Janin, Loutrie . . ."

"Hold it! I don't need that many. Tell them I want a twenty-four-hour watch kept on the apartment of the masseuse Angèle Louette on the Rue Saint-André-des-Arts. They can arrange a schedule to suit themselves. There's no need for them to keep out of sight. Oh, and one other thing. Warn them that she's got a car."

He lay soaking for a long time in the soapy water, while his wife made fresh coffee for him. At about half past nine, he went down into the street, hailed a taxi, and asked the driver to take him to the corner of the Rue Saint-André-des-Arts. Janin was on duty at the door. The Chief Superintendent shook him by the hand.

"I'm going up to see her now, and it's possible that what I have to say to her may send her running for cover."

"Don't worry. I'll keep my eyes open. Neveu and I have got it all worked out. Neither of us particularly wanted to do a long stint, so we're taking turns about every three hours, and tomorrow night Loutrie will give us a hand."

Maigret went upstairs and rang the bell. The door was opened almost at once.

Angèle Louette, still wearing her black suit, was just putting on a hat.

"You again!" she muttered sullenly. "Can't you leave me alone even for one day?"

"Are you going out?"

"What do you think? I'm not in the habit of doing my housework with a hat on."

"I've just got back from Toulon."

"What's that got to do with me?"

"A great deal, I assure you. Your boy friend drove there in his car. I saw him there."

"It's all over between us."

"Oh, no, it's not. He was the one who undertook to negotiate with Giovanni, remember?"

Involuntarily, she gave a start.

"I may as well tell you right away that he didn't pull it off. Your aunt died for nothing. Would you like to know where the revolver is now? It's at the bottom of the Mediterranean, buried heaven knows how many hundreds of fathoms deep.

"Didn't Marcel call to tell you?"

"If he'd phoned to tell me you were coming, I'd have made it my business not to be at home."

"Where are you going now?"

"To Mass, if you must know. And if that surprises you, it's just too bad."

"Kindly listen to me. You are required to appear for interrogation in my office at nine o'clock tomorrow morning. This is an official summons, so please don't be late. I advise you to bring a suitcase, with whatever personal effects you think you might need, including a change of linen. In other words, we may be obliged to detain you for a time."

"You mean I'm going to be arrested?"

"It's a possibility you have to face, although that's going to be decided by the Examining Magistrate and not by me. Just one more thing and then you can go. An hour ago I gave instructions that you were to be kept under supervision for twenty-four hours a day, and this will continue until you arrive at my office tomorrow morning."

"I hate you!"

"That doesn't surprise me."

All the way down the stairs Maigret could hear her pacing up and down the living room, swearing like a trooper.

"Do you know what she looks like?" he asked Janin.

"No."

"She'll be down in a moment. I'll point her out to you."

Ten minutes later she appeared. When she came out and caught sight of the two men standing on the sidewalk opposite, she gave a violent start.

"You shouldn't have any difficulty keeping her in sight. If she ever took up boxing, she'd be in the heavyweight class."

He walked home, enjoying the sunshine in the quiet of a Sunday morning. How would they spend the afternoon, he wondered. Sometimes they went out in the car, with Madame Maigret at the wheel, but, on the whole, she preferred not to drive on a Sunday, especially on the busy roads out of Paris.

Not that it mattered what they did. Even if they only strolled side by side through the streets, they were never bored.

"Your friend Marella telephoned. You just missed him by five minutes. He wants you to call him back at his home as soon as possible. He says he gave you his number."

She looked inquiringly at her husband.

"You don't seem surprised that he should be calling

you on a Sunday morning, when you only saw him last night."

"I was half expecting it."

He put through a call to Toulon. Within a few minutes Marella was on the line.

"Did you have a good trip?"

"Thanks to your local wine, I slept like a baby."

"I suppose you can guess what I called you about."

"What's happened to him?"

"At seven o'clock this morning he was fished out of the harbor."

"Knifed?"

"No. A thirty-eight-caliber bullet right between the eyes."

A silence followed, both men thinking their own thoughts.

"You did your best by advising him to go with you to Paris. But he thought he was smart. He thought that you were lying and that there was still something in it for him."

"No hope of pinning it on Giovanni, I suppose?"

"You can bet your life he's covered his tracks. Probably the killer didn't even know whom he was working for. No doubt he got his instructions from some intermediary whom Giovanni knew he could trust."

"Any ideas?"

"Too many. There are at least twenty men in this area who could have done it. Very likely he got someone from Nice or Cannes or Marseilles. And I'll bet you anything he isn't in Toulon now. He wouldn't be likely to hang around waiting to be recognized."

Marella paused, evidently lost in thought.

"Mind you, we'll catch up with him eventually, but it will probably be in four or five years' time, and for something quite different."

"You don't need to tell me. We have the same problems here. Thanks for letting me know, anyway. Were you there when they emptied his pockets?"

"Yes. Nothing of much interest. Two thousand francs in his wallet, along with his identity card and driver's license. His registration was in the glove compartment of his car, which was left all night outside the Hôtel des Cinq Continents.

"And there was also some small change and a key."

"I'd be grateful if you'd let me have the key."

"I'll mail it to you as soon as I can. I'll take it to the railway station myself. Apart from the items I mentioned, there were a handkerchief, some cigarettes, and a pack of chewing gum."

"Did you go through his suitcase?"

"A black-and-white check suit. Some underwear. No papers. Nothing else, in fact, but a cheap paperback novel with a lurid cover."

"Not even a notebook with telephone numbers?"

"No. But someone may have got to it before me. According to the Police Doctor, he died somewhere around one in the morning. That's only a rough estimate, of course. We won't know for sure until later today, after the autopsy."

"I hope Claudine won't hold it against me."

"Hold what against you?"

"Well, it's because of me that your Sunday morning has been ruined."

"She's in the kitchen. Hold on! She's saying something.

She wants to be remembered to you both. As far as I'm concerned, this is now no more than a routine inquiry, which I'll leave in the hands of my deputy."

"Have you seen Bob again?"

"No. I hope he won't go the same way. I'd be sorry, because he's always played straight with me."

"Surely he's too valuable to Giovanni!"

"So you've been thinking along the same lines as I have. There has to be a go-between linking Giovanni with his pals in the underworld."

"And who better than Bob, wouldn't you say?"

"Have a pleasant Sunday!"

"The same to you. And many thanks for all your help."

Maigret replaced the receiver.

"Bad news?" asked Madame Maigret, noting his worried expression.

"From the professional angle, I suppose I should call it very good news. A petty crook has been murdered in Toulon, thus saving the state an expensive trial. He's been known to us for a long time as a pimp, and over the last months he's been living off a woman of fifty-five. If he wasn't a murderer himself, he was certainly an accomplice."

"Are you talking about the old lady?"

"The old lady in the white hat and gloves, yes."

He could still see her, suddenly stepping into his path on the sidewalk of the Quai des Orfèvres, and looking up at him, her eyes alive with admiration and hope.

She was dead. And now Le Grand Marcel was dead, too, and the object for which the couple had searched so long, the precious revolver, which had been in the bedside-table drawer all the time, was lost and gone forever.

"What are we having for lunch?"

"*Blanquette* of veal."

They sat around until half past twelve. Maigret turned on the radio for the news, though, as he had expected, there was no reference to the murder in Toulon.

"Don't think about her. It's such a lovely day."

"Too lovely to stay shut up indoors, don't you think?"

"Do you have anything particular in mind?"

"We can talk about that as we go."

As always, she took his arm, and they walked toward the Quais. On the Quai de la Mégisserie they went past the pet shop, which, today, had the shutters closed, and stopped for a moment outside the building where the old lady had lived.

"What floor?"

"Second."

"That's going to make someone very happy."

"What do you mean?"

"The people who take her apartment. They'll have one of the finest views in Paris."

They walked on, and, before very long, they were in the Tuileries Gardens.

"Let's sit down for a few minutes," he suggested.

And thus he fulfilled a wish that had been growing on him ever since the previous night. As far as he could remember, this was the first time he had ever sat on a bench in a public park. He had always thought of park benches as serving no useful purpose, unless it was to provide resting places for tramps and lovers.

It took them some time to find an unoccupied bench. All the others were taken, and not only by elderly people. There were a great many young mothers watching their children at play. A man in his thirties was reading a book on biology.

"It's very pleasant here, isn't it?"

Little toy boats with white sails skimmed over the glassy surface of the pond.

"You'll get wet if you don't watch out, Hubert! If you lean over any farther, you'll fall in!"

How restful it was. Seen from here, life seemed very simple and uneventful.

The old lady came here every day of her life, weather permitting. Perhaps, like that other old lady whom they could see over there, she scattered breadcrumbs for the birds, which flocked around her in ever-growing numbers.

"Was it because of her that you brought me here?"

He admitted that it was.

"Besides, I wanted, for once in my life, to see what it felt like to sit on a park bench."

With some warmth, he added:

"Especially with you."

"You haven't got a very good memory!"

"Have we ever sat on a public bench together, then?"

"When we were engaged. It was in the gardens of the Place des Vosges. That was when you kissed me for the first time, as a matter of fact."

"You're absolutely right. My memory must be going. I wouldn't mind kissing you now, but there are really too many people about."

"We're a bit old for that sort of thing, don't you think?"

They decided not to go home for dinner. They went to a restaurant on the Place des Victoires. They liked the food and the atmosphere and enjoyed going there from time to time.

"Shall we eat on the terrace?"

"I wouldn't advise it," interposed the head waiter. "The nights are still quite cold. It's really too early in the year to eat out of doors."

They had sweetbreads, which were delicious, followed by tiny lamb cutlets and, to end with, strawberry tart.

"It's such a rare treat," murmured Madame Maigret.

"What is?"

"Having you to myself for practically the whole day. I'll bet you anything that tomorrow I'll get a message saying you won't be home for lunch."

"Very likely. Almost certainly, in fact. Tomorrow I'll be having a battle of wits with the Sergeant-Major."

"Is that what you call that poor woman?"

"That poor woman, as you call her, probably murdered her aunt."

"It wasn't premeditated, was it?"

"No."

"I suppose, being discovered like that, she completely lost her head."

"Are you trying to defend her?"

"No, but I can't help thinking about her. Didn't you say she was ugly?"

"A woman utterly without charm, at any rate."

"And presumably without charm even as a young girl?"

"Almost certainly, I'd say."

"So, since no man would give her a second look, she had to go about things in a rather different way."

"You would have made a good defense lawyer."

"Fifty-five! You did say she was fifty-five, didn't you? I suppose she thought she'd never get another after Marcel, so she clung to him for dear life."

"She's still clinging. She doesn't know yet what's happened to him."

"Don't you think she'll try to make a run for it?"

"I'm having her watched twenty-four hours a day."

"I wouldn't want to be in your place tomorrow morning."

"I'm not exactly looking forward to it myself."

But it was his job. And Angèle Louette was not the type to inspire much compassion.

Madame Maigret had no difficulty in following her husband's train of thought when he murmured:

"Marella's son has quite made up his mind not to join the Force."

If he himself had had a son, what advice would he have given him?

Arm in arm, they walked back to Boulevard Richard-Lenoir, and, for a long time, neither spoke a word.

Chapter 7

When, on the dot of nine, old Joseph ushered her in, Maigret found himself looking at her in a rather different light. He felt, in her presence, a degree of embarrassment that he had not felt before. Perhaps it was because of what his wife had said the previous night.

He even went so far as to get up to greet her, and, as he did so, it struck him that she looked a little pathetic, with her small overnight bag in her hand.

She was pale, but when had he ever seen her with color in her cheeks? She was ugly. Would he have been equally hard on her if she had been an attractive woman?

"Put your bag down over there, and take a seat."

They were all set to begin. Lapointe, sitting at one end of the desk, was ready and waiting to take shorthand notes of the interview.

"It's just nine, isn't it? I had to miss my eight o'clock appointment, and I had another at nine. You realize, don't you, that you're taking the bread out of my mouth?"

He had already read the reports of his inspectors on her movements yesterday. After returning from Mass, she had stayed in for the rest of the day. There had been lights on in her apartment until far into the night.

No one had been to see her. She had spent the long hours of waiting alone.

Was that why she was looking so very grave, why all the fight seemed to have gone out of her?

He picked up the telephone.

"Please check whether Judge Libart is in."

He heard the telephone ringing in an empty room.

"Not yet, Chief, and his clerk isn't there, either."

"Thank you."

He lit his pipe and said to Angèle Louette:

"Smoke if you want to."

"You're very kind. Granting the last wish of the condemned woman."

"The time has come, mademoiselle, for us to get down to brass tacks. I may have to repeat some of the questions I've already asked you, but I sincerely hope this will be the last time."

A mood of grayness and sullenness seemed to hang over this confrontation. It was reflected even in the weather. For the past two weeks the sun had shone unremittingly, but now the sky was overcast, and a fine drizzle was spattering the streets of Paris.

"I take it you don't deny that your aunt was murdered?"

"The medical evidence seems conclusive."

"Did she have, as far as you know, any enemies?"

"No."

She was calm, in a dull and heavy way, like the weather. Her expression was blank. She was looking composedly at

161

the Chief Superintendent. Whatever her feelings, if any, she was concealing them admirably.

It was as though all those long hours of solitude on Sunday had drained the spirit out of her.

"Any friends?"

"I don't know of any friends, either."

"Did you call on her by appointment?"

"My aunt didn't have a telephone. I tried to persuade her to have one installed, but she wouldn't hear of it."

"Why did you go to see her?"

"Because I was her only relative."

She was wearing the same black suit, as if to convey the impression that she was in mourning.

"You knew, I assume, when you were likely to find her at home?"

"Yes."

"In other words, you were familiar with her routine."

"She was a creature of habit."

"Every morning she went out to do her shopping locally. Isn't that so?"

"That's right."

"And after lunch, if I'm not mistaken, she took a nap in her armchair?"

She nodded.

"Later, weather permitting, she walked to the Tuileries Gardens and stayed there an hour or two sitting on a bench."

"Surely we've been through all this before?"

"I have my reasons for going through it again. You were not fond of your aunt, were you?"

"No."

"You never forgave her, did you, for palming you off with a hundred-franc note when you went to her for help because you were pregnant?"

"It's not the sort of thing one can easily forget."

"Still, you went on going to see her. How many times a year, would you say?"

"I don't remember."

"How many times a month?"

"Once, sometimes twice."

"Always at the same time of day?"

"Nearly always. I finish work at six. And she usually got in around that time in the summer."

"Did she invite you to sit down?"

"I didn't wait to be asked. After all, she was my aunt."

"You were her sole heir?"

"Yes."

"Did you often think about it?"

"I realized it would make things easier for me in my old age. It's harder work being a masseuse than most people realize. It takes a good deal of physical strength. A few more years and I'll be too old for it."

"In the meantime, did you ever ask her for money?"

"Occasionally. In my kind of work there are bound to be slack periods. In the summer, for instance, when all my clients are away from Paris on vacation, some for two or three months."

"Did you ever quarrel with your aunt?"

"Never."

"Did you ever reproach her for her meanness?"

"No."

"Did she know how you felt about her?"

"I suppose so, yes."

"Were you aware that she never kept much money in the apartment?"

"I knew that, yes."

"Who took the wax impression of the lock?"

"I didn't, at any rate."

"Was it your lover?"

"If so, he never told me."

"But he did show you the key he'd had cut?"

"I never saw any key."

"Now, you're lying again. Not only did you have a key to the apartment, you also had a key to your Uncle Antoine's little cubbyhole on the other side of the landing."

She was sulkily silent, like a scolded child.

"I have some bad news for you, I'm afraid. When you've heard it, you may feel inclined to alter your statement."

A flicker of interest animated her face.

"First of all, you may as well admit that there was no quarrel between you and Marcel, and that you did not, as you claim, turn him out."

"Think what you like. I can't stop you."

"All your indignation at his habit of spending half the day in bed was an act, put on for my benefit."

There was no reaction.

"As I told you yesterday, I saw him in Toulon. You, needless to say, knew perfectly well what he had gone there for."

"No."

"You're lying again. A few miles out of Toulon there is a villa belonging to a man by the name of Pepito Giovanni. He's a retired gangster. He's been going straight, more or less, for years, and is now the head of a substantial, and quite legitimate, business empire. Marcel, I imagine, must have worked for him at some time or other, though he probably was only a very small cog in a large machine.

"Marcel could never have been anything more than a petty crook. The most he ever had was a walk-on part."

For an instant the woman's eyes blazed with fury, but she did not speak.

"Do you go along with me, so far?"

"I have nothing to say."

"Excuse me for a moment."

He picked up the receiver again and, this time, was put through to the Examining Magistrate.

"Maigret speaking. May I come up to see you for a moment?"

"Of course, only make it as soon as you can. I have a witness to see in ten minutes."

Leaving Lapointe in charge of his visitor, he walked through the door to the Law Courts.

"How is it going?"

"I don't want to sound overoptimistic, but I hope today will see the end of it. I went to Toulon on Saturday, as a result of which there have been several developments, but I won't bother you with them now.

"What I need at this moment is a warrant for the arrest of Angèle Louette."

"Isn't that the niece?"

"Yes."

"Do you really believe she killed the old lady?"

"I don't know yet, but I will very soon, I hope. Which

is why I'm not sure whether or not I'll need that warrant."

"You heard what the Chief Superintendent said, Gérard. Make out the warrant, will you?"

When Maigret got back to his office, he found the two occupants stiff and silent, like a couple of wax effigies.

He handed the warrant to Angèle.

"I take it you know what this means, and that you now understand why I asked you to bring a few personal things and a change of linen with you?"

She neither stirred nor spoke.

"First, let's talk about Marcel. I found him in a bar in Toulon, the Bar de l'Amiral. It was an old haunt of his when he lived in the South. The barman, Bob, was a close friend of his. Did he ever speak of him?"

Dryly she answered:

"No."

But she was now very much on the alert, and waiting apprehensively for what was to follow.

"A man of Giovanni's standing wouldn't usually have any dealings with small fry like Marcel. An intermediary was required, and that was where Bob came in. I don't know what he said to Giovanni exactly, but it was to the effect that Marcel had something to sell, something very big. It had to be, since the former boss of the underworld agreed to see him the next morning. Do you follow me?"

"Yes."

"You do understand that I'm talking about the revolver?"

"As I've said time and time again, I've never seen the revolver you're referring to."

"And each time you were lying. Giovanni was interested, so much so that he kept the model. I went to see him shortly afterward, and we had a most interesting talk. Among other things I told him where the revolver came from, and also how deeply Marcel was implicated in the murder of your aunt.

"Now, if there's one person more touchy than another about getting mixed up in anything sticky, it's an underworld boss who has made a fortune and virtually retired from criminal activity.

"Giovanni had learned from me that, as long as he was in possession of the gun, he was in grave danger, and I was scarcely through the gates of his house when he boarded his motor launch and roared out to sea.

"And, as a result, your uncle's precious revolver is now lying many fathoms deep on the ocean bed."

Maigret tapped the ashes out of his pipe and filled another.

"But that's not all that happened in Toulon. There were further developments after I left. A colleague of mine there called me soon after I left you yesterday. But before I go into that, are you prepared to repeat your statement that everything was over between you and Marcel, and that you told him, once and for all, that you never wanted to see him again?"

"I'm waiting to hear the rest of your story."

"Marcel himself had become something of a menace. As they say in the trade, dead men tell no tales."

"Is he dead?"

She looked absolutely stricken. Even her voice was scarcely recognizable.

"It's no longer any concern of yours, is it?"

"What happened exactly?"

"He was shot between the eyes in the middle of the

night. With a thirty-eight-caliber gun, which no one but a professional would use. The body was found yesterday morning, floating in the harbor."

"Is this a trap?"

"No."

"Will you swear by everything you hold sacred?"

"I swear."

And then the tears began to roll down her cheeks. She opened her handbag to get out a handkerchief.

Chapter 8

He crossed over to the window, to give her time to recover. The light spring rain was still falling, and glistening umbrellas were to be seen all along the Quai.

He heard her blow her nose, and, when he returned to his seat, she was dabbing a little rouge onto her cheeks.

"So you see, although your aunt paid with her life, it all came to nothing."

She was still snuffling as she got a cigarette from her bag and lit it with a trembling hand.

"All that remains for me to discover is whether it was you or Marcel who smothered the old lady."

Contrary to his expectations, she did not seize the opportunity of putting all the blame on her lover, who was no longer there to defend himself.

"As far as he is concerned, naturally, the case is closed. But that doesn't apply to you."

"Why do you hate me so?"

"I don't hate you. I'm only doing my job, as humanely

as possible, I hope, in the circumstances. You have persistently lied to me, right from the very first. That being so, how else could you expect me to react?"

"You know perfectly well that I loved him."

"I'll go further than that: I believe you still love him, even now that he's dead."

"You're right, I do."

"Why pretend you'd quarreled and parted for ever?"

"That was his idea, to put you off the scent."

"Did you know why he went to Toulon?"

For the first time she looked him straight in the face, without attempting to lie or evade the question.

"Yes."

"How long have you known of the existence of the revolver?"

"Thirteen or fourteen years. I got along very well with my Uncle Antoine. He was a good man, really, but rather lonely, in a way. I don't think my aunt could give him the companionship he'd hoped for. So he spent most of his time shut up in his little cubbyhole."

"And you kept him company?"

"Quite often. He had this overriding passion for gadgets. Scarcely a year went by without his submitting an invention for the Lépine Prize."

"Is that how you knew about the revolver?"

"I watched him work on it for the best part of two years.

" 'There's just one problem I don't seem to be able to overcome,' he told me in confidence. 'If I ever manage to do it, it will go off with quite a bang.'

"And then he burst out laughing.

" 'I don't mean that literally. Quite the contrary, in facı Do you know what a silencer is?'

" 'I've seen them on television and in movies. It's a thing you fit onto the end of a gun, to prevent it from making a noise when it's fired.'

" 'That's it, more or less. Of course you can't just go into a shop and buy one. It's against the law. But suppose you could do away with the silencer as a separate piece of the equipment, by incorporating it into the design of the gun itself?'

"He sounded tremendously excited.

" 'I'm very nearly there. There are just one or two small adjustments to be made. Then I'll register the patent, and in a few years all firearms, including those of the armed forces and the police, will be silent.' "

She sat musing for a little while and then said:

"A few days after that, he died. I know nothing about firearms, and I forgot all about his precious revolver."

"When did you mention it to Marcel?"

"About a month ago. No, less than that, three weeks ago. We were walking across the Pont-Neuf, and I pointed out my aunt's apartment on the Quai de la Mégisserie. I mentioned that I would be inheriting some money from her one of these days."

"What made you say that?"

She flushed and looked away.

"I didn't want to lose him."

She cherished no illusions.

"A few minutes later we stopped for a drink at an open-air café, when I suddenly remembered the revolver. I told him the story, and, to my amazement, he seemed terrifically excited about it.

" 'Did you ever see the gun after your uncle died?'

" 'No. I've never been in his workshop since then.'

" 'Did your aunt know about it?'

" 'He may have mentioned it to her, but I doubt if she ever gave it a second thought, any more than I did. I'll ask her.'

" 'No, don't do that. Don't even mention it.

" 'Do you have a key to the apartment?'

" 'No.'

" 'And this room you call the cubbyhole, does it have a separate key?'

" 'Yes, but I don't know where my aunt keeps it. Maybe in her bag.'

"It was several days before he mentioned the matter again. One evening, when I got home, he was standing there with two keys in his hand.

" 'What are you going to do?'

" 'Find the revolver.'

" 'What for?'

" 'Don't you realize it's worth a fortune! I want you to go to your aunt's sometime when you know she's out, and search every room in the apartment and the workshop.'

" 'What's the point? It will all come to me eventually anyway.'

" 'Women like her have a very strong grip on life. You may have to spend another ten years massaging women, all over Paris, before you see a penny.' "

She looked at Maigret and sighed.

"Now do you understand? At first I refused to have anything to do with it, but he just wouldn't let it drop, and I was afraid of losing him. In the end, I agreed. One afternoon I took the keys and went to the Quai de la Mégisserie. I saw my aunt set off for the Tuileries, and I knew she wouldn't be back before six.

"First I searched the apartment. I went through every drawer and looked in every possible place where I thought it might be hidden. And then I put everything carefully back as it was before."

"Not quite carefully enough, though. She knew someone had been there."

"Two days later I searched the workroom. In all, I went to the Quai de la Mégisserie four times."

"And Marcel?"

"Just the once."

"When was that?"

Once more she turned her head away.

"On the afternoon of my aunt's death."

"What did he say when he got back to your apartment?"

"I wasn't there. I had an appointment with a client at half past five. She kept me waiting. The client is someone I've been giving massages to for the best part of twenty years. She's Madame de la Roche, of Sixty-one Boulevard Saint-Germain."

"What time did you get home?"

"At seven. As usual, she kept me gossiping."

"Why didn't you tell me you had an alibi?"

"That would have been as good as to accuse Marcel."

"And you preferred to let me go on suspecting you?"

"As long as you didn't know which of us it was . . ."

"So the gun was hidden, for a time, on top of your wardrobe."

"Yes."

"And it was your lover who found it in the bedside-table drawer?"

"Yes. It's the last place I'd have thought of looking for it. My aunt was scared stiff of firearms."

"Have you got all that, Lapointe? Just call to check with Madame de la Roche, Boulevard Saint-Germain, and then you can start typing."

Left alone with her in his office, Maigret felt oppressed. He got up and went over to the window.

"As far as Marcel is concerned," he mumbled, "the case is closed. You can't prosecute a dead man. You, on the other hand, are very much alive. It's true that you had no hand in the death of the old lady, assuming your alibi is confirmed."

She was no longer the same woman, sitting there before his desk, facing his empty chair. All the stiffening had gone out of her. Her face was crumpled in misery, her shoulders drooping.

Five long minutes of silence passed before Lapointe came back into the room.

"The lady confirms her story" was all he said.

"Thanks."

"Do you realize the position you're in at this moment?"

"You showed me the warrant. I realize what it means."

"When I had the warrant drawn up, I didn't know whether it was you or Marcel who had smothered your aunt."

"Well, you know now."

"You were not present at the time. It was an unpremeditated crime, so you couldn't possibly have foreseen that it was going to happen. In other words, you are not implicated in the murder itself. Where you did wrong was in shielding your lover and in concealing on your premises a stolen firearm."

She looked at him blankly. It was as though she had lost all interest in life. She seemed to be miles away; in Toulon perhaps, with Marcel?

174

Maigret went across and opened the door of the inspectors' duty room. Fat Torrence happened to be the one nearest him.

"Come into my office a minute, will you? Stay here till I get back, and don't let the lady go."

"Right, Chief."

Once more he climbed the stairs to the Examining Magistrates' floor. Judge Libart was interviewing a witness, but he sent him out for a few minutes so that Maigret could have a word with him in private.

"Did she do it?"

"No. She's got an alibi as solid as a rock."

Maigret told him the whole story as briefly as possible. Nevertheless, it took him quite some time.

"There doesn't seem much point in going after Giovanni," he murmured, in conclusion.

"It wouldn't do any good."

"If you consider the matter carefully, she's no more guilty than he is."

"You mean . . ."

The judge scratched his head.

"That is what you have in mind, isn't it? To let her go scot free?"

It would never do to admit that it was Madame Maigret who, indirectly at least, had put the idea into his head.

"First of all, we've got to prove that she was a party to the theft. And that won't be easy, especially now that the revolver has disappeared."

"I see your point."

It was another quarter of an hour before Maigret got back to his office, because, in the meantime, the Examining Magistrate had taken him off to see the Public Prosecutor.

The Chief Superintendent could not help being a little shocked at finding Torrence seated behind his desk in his own personal armchair.

"She hasn't moved a muscle, Chief."

"Did she say anything?"

"She never opened her mouth. Can I go now?"

Angèle looked at Maigret without interest. She seemed to be resigned to her fate.

"How old are you, exactly?"

"Fifty-six. I don't tell everyone, mind you, because some of my clients might begin to think I was past it."

"Which of the two apartments do you intend to live in, yours or your aunt's?"

She stared at him in amazement.

"Have I any choice in the matter?"

Deliberately, he picked up the warrant and tore it in half.

"You're free to go," he said simply.

She did not get to her feet immediately. For a moment, it seemed as though she didn't have the strength. Tears rolled down her cheeks, but she made no attempt to wipe them away.

"I don't . . . I have no words. . . ."

"There's nothing more to be said. I'd be obliged if you'd come back sometime this afternoon to sign your statement."

She got up, hesitated for a moment, then went slowly toward the door.

He called after her:

"Your suitcase!"

"Yes, of course. I'd forgotten all about it."

But there was so much that she would never forget.

Épalinges
May 7, 1970